D1528150

The Horse Talker

The Horse Talker

by Jeanne Williams

AN AUTHORS GUILD BACKINPRINT.COM EDITION

AN AUTHORS GUILD BACKINPRINT.COM EDITION

Published by iUniverse.com, Inc.

For information address:
iUniverse.com, Inc.
5220 S 16th, Ste. 200
Lincoln, NE 68512
www.iuniverse.com

Originally published by Prentice Hall

ISBN: 0-595-09587-9

Printed in the United States of America

FOR WILL

"Be Happy In Your Work."

Contents

The Horse Talker

🝤 🝤 🝤 *Splintered Lance*

Lan sat facing the sunset, trying to be as still as the mesquite limb he had thrust into the ground a few feet away, but both his legs had gone to sleep from keeping that position so long. He either had to get up or fall over.

Stealthily, as if the very rocks might curl their faces at a would-be warrior who needed to stretch, Lan pushed to his feet. He sighed with pain and relief as blood throbbed through his cramped feet and legs, but his head swam till he had to catch hold of an outcrop of rock. The sun was leaving him on this third day of his vigil in his search for medicine.

He had not eaten during that time. He had prayed, watched, and smoked his pipe as all young Comanche men were counseled to do at this most important of trials. But no spirit had come to him. No magic bird had called, nor furred beast spoken.

Could it be that no creature wished to give him its power? Did they know he was really white, and scorn him as Yellow Wolf had said they would? Lan pushed away from the rock, stood on his own legs though they tried to reel under him. He could not leave this hill without medicine, some sign from the spirit that would be his guardian.

Of course, just meeting Yellow Wolf on his way out of the village had gotten Lan off to the worst possible start on his search for power. Stripped to breechclout and moccasins,

1

equipped with the necessary buffalo robe, pipe, tobacco, steel and flint, Lan had felt gravely proud and expectant as he told Swift Otter, his mother, good-by. He had been sure a spirit would claim and bless him at his vigil by his father's burial place on the hill. But that certainty had been rudely shattered when Yellow Wolf stepped into his path.

"Hai, Bloody Scalp, where are you going? The spirits will see your blue eyes and look through your skin to the white blood. You won't see anything—unless it's Big Cannibal Owl." Glancing about to be sure the other young braves and maidens were admiring his wit—especially Shining Mirror, the pretty daughter of Thunder Waters—Yellow Wolf made a terrible face and flapped his arms. "Aren't you afraid he'll eat you?"

A laugh went up from the boys and Shining Mirror tittered. Big Cannibal Owl was used to frighten bad children. Lan dived for Yellow Wolf, but the other had side-stepped, stretching out a foot that sent Lan sliding into the dust.

Stumbling up amidst howls of amusement, Lan started for his enemy, but Thunder Waters, peace chief since the death of Lan's father, had stepped between. He put the buffalo robe bundle into Lan's arms.

"This is no way to start your hunt for medicine," the old man warned. The grooves in his face were like marks in granite. "Go your way and be humble before the spirits."

Lan, still furious, gnawed his lip, but boys did not argue with Thunder Waters. Thanking the peace chief, Lan moved off, avoiding the troubled gaze of his mother who had been drawn from her *tipi* by the confusion. It was small help to hear Thunder Waters reprove Yellow Wolf. "A warrior should not make jest of a lad who goes to find his power."

"I tried only to save him disappointment." Yellow Wolf's disagreeable voice was pitched high to reach Lan. "That torch-head of his would frighten the toughest bull buffalo spirit. And still using that name he called himself as a baby—a white baby! He should be a slave like the other captives."

Thunder Waters' reply came faintly to Lan's burning ears. "You know, Yellow Wolf, that Lan is neither slave nor captive. He had not more than three summers when he became the son of Swift Otter and Arrow In His Shield."

Those were the last human words Lan had heard. Now, during his lonely watch, he clung to them. Arrow In His Shield was buried in the crevice a few yards away, sitting upright, facing the rising sun, in the place where years ago he had received his medicine.

Valiant warrior in his prime, peace chief and medicine man in life's twilight, Arrow In His Shield was all any boy could dream of becoming. With a surge of humiliation, Lan hoped that in the spirit world where his father hunted undiminishing herds through perpetually balmy weather, Arrow In His Shield did not know and sorrow for the failure of his adopted son. Lan pulled himself tall, fixing his eye on the mesquite limb to which he had given the meaning of a *pukutsi's* tether.

Lan had never seen one of these fantastically courageous warriors, but Arrow In His Shield, during a long life, had known two, and used to tell about them, in tones half-pitying, half-admiring. Called by some tribes "Crazy Dogs Wishing To Die," these braves did everything in a mad, contrary fashion just backwards to usual behavior. In battle they did not fight. The *pukutsi* would fasten his sash to the ground with an arrow, and there he was expected to remain, singing his songs, till he was killed or a friend released him. *Pukutsis* were admired, but a man seldom became one unless his life through grief or trouble had become a burden to him and a glorious death seemed welcome. It was in this desperate spirit that Lan had tethered himself on the hill. As the third night, thick and purple, closed in about him, Lan got out his pipe, the old straight one made of

3

deer's shank-bone. Arrow In His Shield used to carry it on expeditions. Wrapped with sinew from the back of a buffalo's neck, the pipe was much stronger than the fancier stemmed ones—the right sort of pipe, Lan felt, to use on a medicine quest. He tipped a little tobacco into it. The People, as Comanches called themselves, got tobacco from the Mexican traders who also sold them metal arrowheads, cookpots, and ammunition. Swift Otter had cut and pounded the long leaves to shreds, mixing in crushed sumac leaves. Though Comanches smoked for pleasure as well as ceremonially, there was always something solemn about it.

Facing south, seeing both east and west, Lan prayed to the Great Spirit. *Father, help me. Bring me a vision. Do not deny me power because I am white-born. I cannot remember when I was not in the lodge of Swift Otter and Arrow In His Shield. Only my eyes remember and my hair. Father, if I go home without medicine, Yellow Wolf will mock me. Surely some spirit would bless me if You say I am truly Comanche.*

A rustling came from the brush. Breath pushing out his chest, Lan froze. Slowly, he turned.

Nothing. Even the sound was gone. Sick with despair and hunger, Lan fought a stinging in his eyes. He went to the spring, filled his mouth with the lukewarm trickle, and drank till the pangs in his stomach eased. He grinned a little. Funny, to be able to fool your stomach that way. Maybe he could be asleep before it found out he had filled it with water instead of good meat.

On the ledge below the stone-piled burial mound of his father, Lan wrapped up in the robe and lay down, careful to face east and cover his head. At dawn he would wake and pray again, absorbing the rays of the morning-strong sun. That would be the fourth day.

Usually if a vision had not come by then, the boy went home and tried later when he felt the spirits might be more generous. But Lan dreaded defeat because he was afraid it would be repeated. In bone and flesh he was not of The People. He was born from those strange harsh-bearded creatures he had seen once at a parley with the blue-coats.

Disgust at this flooded him. He rubbed at his skin as if he could change its color. All right, he was nobody! He would have to show what he was. And he would, oh, how proudly and bravely he would, if only some spirit would be his guardian!

Maybe he would have had better luck if he had gone to Sun Bluff where Yellow Wolf and many other boys had found their medicine. Lan shrugged the disloyal thought away. The spirit of Arrow In His Shield would have helped if it could. It was Lan's own fault—the fault, rather, of hair red as new fire, and the strange eyes. In quiet pools Lan had seen them, the color of clouds which brought bitter storms across the *Llano Estacado,* or Staked Plains, the level tableland to the west. Swift Otter, still graceful and slim as the girl who had earned that name for her diving, thought his hair was pretty. With her quick fingers, she liked to plait it and weave in bits of yarn and feathers. She was proud of Lan's peculiarities.

But what if he got no power? Yellow Wolf's mother already liked shrilly to remind Swift Otter that *her* son had received medicine his very first night on Sun Bluff. A wolf had appeared and given him magic and songs. That was almost two years ago, and Yellow Wolf had grown more unbearable each day, swelled with successes.

Besides several raids on the Texan settlements, Yellow Wolf had stolen horses from the blue-coat Fort two days' ride to the southeast. He had killed the buffalo whose hides made his private *tipi* and he possessed a breech-loading carbine. Though young men could not publicly favor a certain girl, he seemed to please the village's prettiest maiden, Shining Mirror, very well. All in all, Yellow Wolf was the showiest brave in camp. He probably would not have noticed Lan except for one thing.

Lan could tame horses better than anyone among his people. With voice and breath and some touch of the hands he was born with and could not have explained, Lan could master horses already named outlaws and marked for slaughter next time meat ran short. When some warriors had an especially fine horse they wanted tamed without spirit-breaking cruelty, they brought him to Lan.

Yellow Wolf broke horses as if he were in battle with them, as if the beasts were enemies. He choked them down, flogged them, yanked them about by the hackamore. Thunder Waters had rebuked him for this before some of the men, pointing out that Lan trained horses without ruining them. Yellow Wolf could not bear to be excelled in anything by anybody, certainly not by a white waif. His hounding of Lan had reached its peak in that insult as Lan started out of the village on his medicine quest.

To go back now without a vision, face Yellow Wolf's jeering eyes and Swift Otter's sad ones . . .

I won't! Lan vowed, breathing the stale hot air under the buffalo robe. He resisted the urge to slip it back and draw in air as clean and fresh and cooling as water. *I've put the limb up like a pukutsi's pledge and I'll stay here till I win. Maybe I'll be a pukutsi when I grow up. Then if I get killed in battle, Swift Otter will be proud and my comrades will see that she lives well. They will give her always a share of their war loot out of love of me because I was brave.*

Lan roused suddenly, all at once. A moist, cool something nuzzled at his cheek. The medicine spirit!

An awed thrill ran through his blood, prickling at his scalp and spine. Was it Coyote, that best friend of all to man? Or fox, or deer? Would it speak to him in human words?

What should he say? Whatever spirit it was, he did not want to frighten or estrange it with undue haste. He had to prove himself worthy of its favor, show that although he was white, he had the control and temper of one of The People.

Keeping his face immobile, Lan opened his eyes. He gazed into the flickering gaze of Yellow Wolf. In the bright moonlight the young brave loomed tall. His mouth curved in a contemptuous grin.

Lan stared from that face to the stick in Yellow Wolf's hand. It was the make-believe *pukutsi* lance, wrapped at one end with a bit of dampened leather. That was what had felt like the inquisitive nose of some animal guardian.

A red haze shut out Yellow Wolf from Lan's vision for a moment. The muscles in his thighs and legs swelled to leap. But even in his blind rage Lan remembered he was near the burial place of his father. Clenching his fists against the earth, he drove words from the thick swelling mass in his throat.

"What has come to Yellow Wolf that he interrupts a medicine watch?" he asked.

"Coyote will bay the moon into his jaws before you get power," Yellow Wolf said, snapping the stick so that it splintered. "I have come to do you a favor, Bloody Scalp. You can go back with honor instead of skulking in tomorrow night with nothing to show but your shriveled belly and light head. I am going to steal the best horse of the blue-coat chief. I will let you go with me."

The head-soldier's horse! Lan clamped his lips tight on the flood of questions. Horse-capture was a high form of glory. Indeed, sometimes a warrior stole horses in preference to taking scalps. The more dangerous the conditions, the better. To help catch a prize such as the blue-coat chief's horse would wipe out the failure of Lan's medicine search. But why was Yellow Wolf running such a risk? And why did he offer Lan this chance to win praise?

"Why does Yellow Wolf go horse-hunting in the middle of

the night?" Lan asked warily. "Who is with you? Why must you have the horse of the soldiers' chief?"

Yellow Wolf spoke with elaborate patience. "If we go now we can be at the fort in the hours before dawning tomorrow night. Two stand a better chance on such a mission than a crowd. And I need the horse as a bride-price for Thunder Waters' daughter. He does not want me for a son-in-law, so he set what he thought was an impossible price."

That made sense as far as it went. Lan's horse-talking gift was sure to have something to do with it, too. Still—

"You do not like me," Lan said. "Why pick me to go?"

For an instant, Yellow Wolf lost his superior smile. A steel-hard glint showed in his narrowed eyes. "I will speak truth, Bloody Scalp. You are right that I have no love for you. But you have more skill with horses than any of The People. I must have this horse for Thunder Waters. I do not want it to squeal or make an alarm. So I need you. And you need me! Unless you want to go back to the village like a whipped cur and answer questions about the spirit you did not meet." Lan glanced towards the splintered limb he had thrust into the ground with such fierce, hopeful intention.

"I might have found power today," he growled, "if you had not come up here."

"You find power?" Yellow Wolf watched Lan with real, though scornful pity. "You, a white?"

Lan flushed. He got up, holding himself very straight, so that he stood even a bit taller than Yellow Wolf. "Arrow In His Shield is my father. Swift Otter is my mother."

"Of course!" Yellow Wolf passed his hand over his face in mock confusion. "You got your hair from the sunset and your eyes from the hail clouds." His tone roughened with entreaty and threat. "Listen, Bloody Scalp. The spirits will not come to you. You must earn glory in other ways. Help me now and when

8

we come back with the blue-coat chief's horse, no one will think much of your failure in the medicine search."

Lan turned. He looked towards his father's grave, at the heaped rocks. A great flood of loneliness, of being separate and unproved, swept over him. Yellow Wolf was right. He must show that he had a Comanche heart before the spirits or The People would accept him. If he helped capture the prized horse of the blue-coat chief he would not have to go back to the village in humiliation.

"Why do you ponder, Bloody Scalp? Are you afraid?"

"No," said Lan, facing the other youth. "But I have no supplies for an expedition, and no horse."

"I brought one for you, and provisions."

In the east, faint pink streaks were beginning, though in the western heavens the moon was still high and ghostly bright. Lan took a deep breath.

"I will go with you."

Yellow Wolf moved off at once down the slope. "Come!" he said impatiently when Lan, hunger-weakened, lagged a bit. "Thunder Waters plans to move the camp soon for the buffalo hunting. We must get back from the Fort before then." As if temptation might make Lan walk faster, Yellow Wolf added, "After we get the chief's great white horse, you may steal one for your own prize if it's handy. Hurry, will you? Hasn't living with The People taught you how to pick up your feet?"

Lan cleared his head with a determined shake. He got to the bottom of the slope a few seconds ahead of Yellow Wolf and laughed softly, not caring if the other heard him.

Maybe he was white. But to whom had Yellow Wolf come for help in stealing the blue-coat chief's favorite horse? Climbing into the saddle of the extra mount, Lan picked up the hair bridle. He rode with his enemy, who needed him and whom he needed, heading southeast toward the Fort on the river called by Mexicans the Rio Grande. To Mexicans and blue-coat soldiers it formed some kind of border, Lan vaguely knew. And this amused him. For there were no borders to a Comanche. From the Arkansas River far north, from the Cross Timbers to the east, from the western settlements of New Mexico, the vast lands of the country the Comanches considered their own stretched undivided and free. *Comanchería,* the South Plains. And The People were its lords.

To be one of them was worth any danger. Worth, even, putting up with Yellow Wolf. Lan reached into the pouch tied to the pommel and drew out a strip of jerky. He had hoped for pemmican, but that was Yellow Wolf for you!

⚑ ⚑ ⚑ *Mesteñeros*

When their shadows fell straight beneath their horses' hoofs, Yellow Wolf slowed his pinto and spoke for the first time since they left the slope.

"There's a water hole not far from here in the dead river bottom. We'll stop there to drink and rest, for we must ride all night."

Lan nodded. Eating the dry jerky had completely parched his mouth, and they had no water with them. He had noticed that Yellow Wolf's food pouch held considerably more than his own did, but had decided not to argue about it. If he got hungry, he would just insist on more food. Right now all he wanted was water—the most brackish, stinking bitter kind of a drink would do, so long as it was wet.

It was not much farther to the water hole. Lan remembered stopping there once when the village was moving. He looked around, trying to take his mind off his consuming thirst.

The surroundings did not help much. This was the harshest part of a cruel country. Cacti, greasewood and *lechuguilla* scratched tortured silhouettes in the white-hot distance. Yucca and maguey reached imploringly to sky that had forgotten the grace of rain. Far to the west shimmered the foothills which seemed to move and change shape.

It had been near this place that Arrow In His Shield, twelve years ago, had found a wagon. When he had ridden close to investigate, a red-thatched child had poked his head out of the canvas and tried to drive him off. A lump rose in Lan's throat as he seemed to hear his Indian father telling the story, chuckling at the memory.

"Like a wolf-cub you stood there, not afraid though all your kin were dead of the plague. You yelled and poked your stick at me. That was when I wanted you for my son. I used medicine to protect us from the sickness and brought you home to your mother, Swift Otter. I wished to give you a new name, but she liked the one you called yourself so I did not care. The Great Spirit took me to that wagon. He saw you needed a father as much as I needed a son."

And Lan had been their son, tagging after his adored father, learning all skills from him except that horse-talk gift which seemed inborn, and always conscious of Swift Otter's warm love. But being someone's—anyone's—son was not enough when one grew up, Lan knew.

He must be in and of himself; have power, his own special medicine. Till he did, Yellow Wolf and the other braves were right to make sport of him.

Yellow Wolf shaded his eyes with his hand. "The water should be near." Lan noticed that the older boy's lips were puffed and cracking. "Three peaks are far behind it to the west."

Lan thought of water. He tried hastily to forget it—damp delicious cool in the throat, on his tongue.

The sun sucked relentlessly at their bodies, drying the sweat before it formed. Lan felt like that jerked beef which still leathered his mouth with its taste.

It actually hurt to see those pale hills, far and cool as the ice that at times pelted the *Llano*. They danced before Lan's gaze, distorted by the spiraling miles of heat. Then, rising like a sky-chief's *tipi*, three peaks emerged into view.

"There they are!" Lan cried. He dropped his gaze to the bend ahead in the river's dried course. A sort of spiral-walled enclosure was built at the bend; it was too far to tell much about it. But those tiny moving figures could only be men. A lot of them.

Yellow Wolf had seen, too.

"Hai! *Mesteñeros!* They've made a corral by the water hole."

Of course. Lan remembered having seen these brush pens before. They were built where wild horses were apt to come, usually at watering places. The mustangers were mostly Mexican and were known to be as hardy and free-living as Comanches, strays from their civilized brothers.

"Maybe," Lan suggested, "if we rode in and said we wanted to drink and water our horses—"

"Your blood is white as well as your skin," Yellow Wolf snapped. "And the sun has boiled away such brains as you may have had! There is no *mesteñero* on these plains who would not kill the two of us and collect bounty on our scalps. We must wait till the Rio."

The Rio! Why, that was the rest of today and most of the night! Lan's body screamed with thirst and his own wish to take a chance on the hospitality of the *mesteñeros.* But Yellow Wolf was leading this expedition. They were bound to each other as much as if they had been a war party of dozens.

So Lan followed the lead of the older boy, riding over the slope to be out of view when they passed the camp. They rode at some distance from the dry river, but at the rise of a hill that looked down on the mustangers, Yellow Wolf halted.

Jealously, the boys screwed their eyes down at the water hole, and the men who had taken it over. There were at least fifteen of them, lounging in the scant shade, playing cards or busying themselves with equipment.

They were after a big catch, it seemed. The corral was large enough to hold several hundred horses and the stumps of mesquite showed that more than just finger-breadth saplings had been used to build the strong fence, though it was thoroughly disguised with brush. Two crossed sticks lashed together, like those sometimes seen on white men's graves, rose above the entrance. Yellow Wolf tried to spit.

"If we could wait on night, we'd show them some fun," he said. "We'd run off their riding horses and take a few scalps."

"That's fine talk." It hurt to make words, but Yellow Wolf's boasting raised the hackles of Lan's neck. "But these *mesteñeros* stay alive on the plains. You would find their scalps fastened pretty tight to their heads, I think."

Yellow Wolf slanted his mouth downwards in a mocking gibe. "Maybe *you* can't fool a mustanger, but a Comanche could."

"That would depend on the mustanger—and the Comanche. Thunder Waters says that the best *mesteñero* on these plains was once a captive among us."

"You mean the one who became Thunder Waters' blood brother and then repaid The People by running away?" Yellow Wolf laughed grimly. "He had better stay out of the path of Comanches or he'll get what he deserves for his treachery."

"What treachery?" Lan could not really understand how anyone lucky enough to be made Thunder Waters' blood brother and adopted into the tribe could ever want to change, but he wanted to argue with Yellow Wolf. "He didn't hurt anybody. He just went off and never came back. It is said he suffered much when he was first captured. His brothers cried out at the tomahawks and so were killed. But Small Man did not beg. Perhaps he had some medicine."

"He wore the cross, like most Mexicans. But so did his brothers, whom we killed."

"*You* didn't kill them," Lan scoffed. "You were still on your cradleboard."

Yellow Wolf glared, but it was too hot for more squabbling.

"Do you think," asked Lan, "that there could be another water hole on the river bed?"

"I've never seen one, but we can follow it and watch."

They kept behind the low backbone of the ridge till they were well out of sight of the corral. Then they dropped back to the river's edge, scanning the white-yellow clay for some hint of water.

"Dry as old buffalo bones," Yellow Wolf grumbled after a while. "I wish we were a big war party! We'd teach those *mesteñeros* to take over the water holes!"

"You might as well wish we had the blue-coat chief's horse safe back at our village," Lan said. From the corner of his eye, trained from babyhood to catch the slight motions on which an outdoor dweller's life could depend, he glimpsed something far down the river bed at the same time his ears picked up the pound of hoofs.

Yellow Wolf had heard, too. He whirled his horse behind a thicket. Lan urged his mount into another tangle. He did not know exactly what was coming, but the fast, hard beat in the earth echoed through him till his pulse kept the driving, building rhythm.

A white horse sped down the old water course, mane and tail streaming like a warrior's plumes. He was no scrub, no sheep-headed, rough-haired creature like many of the wild horses. Nobly chested, with clean, steel-muscled legs, the stallion was perhaps sixteen hands high—quite the handsomest, fastest horse Lan had ever seen.

All his Indian breeding, with the conviction that a man is only as good as the horse that carries him, rose in Lan. But a new thunder in the packed clay kept him in his hiding.

Two riders, stirrup to stirrup, tore down the way. They had ropes out and rode with a fierce, part-of-the-horse excellence that could not have been matched anywhere. The smaller black horse pulled slightly beyond the claybank.

15

With a tingle of shock, Lan realized that the black's rider was a girl—a girl whose black hair whipped back from a knot of red ribbon as her buckskin-clad figure crouched low over her horse's neck. The other horseman was a dark, slim boy of about Lan's age whose silver-mounted saddle struck glints from the sun.

They aren't Comanches—but they ride as well! Lan was roused out of his staring wonder by Yellow Wolf's sudden shouldering of his rifle, aiming it towards the white stallion's pursuers.

Lan charged from the brush, grabbing Yellow Wolf's hand. "Don't! Fool, do you want to bring the mustangers after us?"

"We have a head start." Yellow Wolf's eyes were glazed with a yellowish film and his chest heaved with excitement. "Two fine scalps—" And he tried to shake Lan off.

That pair of wind-riders dead? The girl's long hair to hang from Yellow Wolf's lance or decorate his shield? Lan could not explain why that seemed horrible to him, and was even ashamed of his feeling. So he convinced himself that his only objection was the one he now gave Yellow Wolf.

"What sort of warrior forgets his quest when some new scent blows across his path? Are we dogs? We cannot get those mustangers after us if we intend to take the blue-coat chief's horse!"

Yellow Wolf wrenched loose. He glared after the vanishing horses. His voice was heavy with malice as he thrust his rifle into its scabbard.

"You looked with delight on the girl and boy. That is because your blood is like theirs. You are no Comanche."

"I have no wish to be a dead one. How could we escape the *mesteñeros* with our horses so thirsty and tired?"

Yellow Wolf shrugged angrily, but kneed his mount on the way again. Lan rode with his eyes on the slashed layers of the river bed; yellow, gray, white—drab, dull colors of thirst.

The three days of his fasting combined with thirst to make him dizzy-headed. Several times he caught the pommel to stay in the saddle. His eyelids drooped against the oblique rays of the westering sun.

At first he saw fuzzy hot red, but this dimmed finally into blackness and crystal—an ice prairie ringed by white peaks where a silver stallion paced cool and distant as the stars and high winds blew. Out of this escape he was roused by Yellow Wolf's guttural voice.

"The Rio is close now. Watch that you don't stumble into it."

Lan jerked erect. He rubbed his eyes.

The moon, bright as the stallion of his thirst-dream, was hanging at the top of the western bowl of sky. They had ridden out most of the night. And they were at the river below the Fort!

His horse snuffed, its head raised. The racking gait smoothed into an eager trot. "He smells the water," whispered Lan. But thirsty as he was, Lan spared a glance over his shoulder.

Some distance off, ghostly and blue-white, lay the Fort. At least Lan supposed that was what the spread of tents and buildings had to be. His horse's rapid descent made him brace himself to keep from sliding down its neck. In a few seconds, hoofs splashed water. Lan slid from the saddle.

Full length in the slow-flowing river, he lay and drank, filling his mouth over and over, sloshing his head and neck. Yellow Wolf was doing the same. Trained in abstemiousness and aware of the dangers of foundering, both boys got up when their first driving need was quenched. They led their horses to the bank.

"We can rest and eat," Yellow Wolf decided. "Then we will let the horses drink again before we start for the Fort."

Lan chewed the parched corn as he spread out to give his cramped body all the comfort possible in this short pause. Jerky, tough and tasteless as an old hide, finished the meal. The moon was sinking fast. In a tantalizingly brief time they had to water their horses, snatch a last drink for themselves, and go back up the bank.

"We'll leave our horses above the Fort," Yellow Wolf said. "Then we'll pick them up on the way home."

If they lived! Looking towards the Fort, its concentration of tents, huts, and buildings which housed several hundred of the blue-coats, Lan's heart swelled and seemed to freeze.

For the first time he felt the danger of what they meant to do. The moon that would help them locate the horse would also betray them if a sentinel happened along. If a dog barked, if the horse put up a struggle, if— This was crazy, desperate!

Lan swung on Yellow Wolf. He was going to pour out his feelings, demand they give up the theft. But the warrior's face, tense yet smiling, alert and confident, stopped the words.

The danger, the difficulty, was exactly why stealing an enemy's horse was considered a coup which could be counted along with war honors. The more risk, the more glory. Lan, watching Yellow Wolf, hated his own white blood which made him weak, and set his teeth.

He would do his part. Of course, the horse was for a bride-price, but Lan would share in the honor. That, a place among The People, was what he wanted now above all things. He pointed to a clearing in a small draw.

"Can't we leave the horses here?"

Yellow Wolf scanned the terrain. He could not see a better place, so he nodded grudgingly. "All right." It must have been hard on him, Lan thought with a private grin, to have to be reasonably agreeable to a person he despised.

They dismounted, trailing the reins. The horses would wander a bit to graze, but would not stray off. Avoiding thorns and cactus, the boys moved cautiously through the flats towards the slumbering Fort.

"It is said by the Mexican traders that this horse is kept in a pen near the blue-coat chief's lodge," said Yellow Wolf. "It is white and the chief had it sent from across the big waters on a huge raft. It is said the chief loves it more than his wife."

Lan saw nothing unusual in that. Some Comanches loved a special horse so dearly that they killed whoever killed it just as they would, with The People's approval, avenge the death of a brother. Killing a man's favorite horse was considered almost as bad as murdering his brother. When one Comanche was asking damages from another who had wronged him, it was customary to demand the accused's best horse.

Now, stealing through the brush, Lan felt an unexpected, hastily-denied thrill of sympathy for the blue-coat chief, who was about to lose the creature he loved. But there were other horses. Besides, the blue-coats were enemies.

"I don't think," Lan ventured, "that it's as fine a horse as that big white we saw the *mesteñeros* after."

"Maybe not. But it is the price Thunder Waters demands for—" Yellow Wolf's voice changed. "For his daughter," he concluded. Lan had a feeling the other boy had started to say something quite different. A kind of uneasiness stirring, Lan shot a searching glance at his companion.

"I didn't know you wanted to marry Thunder Waters' daughter. And you're young to marry at all. Do your parents like the idea?"

"Why shouldn't they?" Yellow Wolf returned haughtily. "I do not tell my private affairs to the village, but if I don't marry Shining Mirror soon, an older man will, for she is sixteen. Your white blood shows in your questions—prying at things that aren't your business!"

"It's my business when I may get killed at it," Lan retorted.

They moved on to the Fort, silent as they came within possible earshot. No lights burned except for one in the single frame building that stood before the hollow square in the middle of the place. A guard moved before the lighted window, passed on down the row of grass-roofed adobe houses. Most of the Fort's people evidently lived in the tents that spread behind the adobes on all sides of the square.

"The place with the light must be the camp of the chief," muttered Yellow Wolf. "See the corral out back of it? His pet horse should be there. Be careful, Bloody Scalp! There may be more than one sentry."

Slipping across the space between the wilderness and the lighted building, the boys could see through the window. A man with gray hair sat at a table working over some papers. He had a curling beard, the first Lan had seen, though he had heard of them.

Yellow Wolf nudged Lan, patted his own chin and head. "Two coups," he joked, pointing at the white man. Lan crept on towards the corral.

Like all boys, he had had glory-dreams of taking trophies; but the pleasant glow did not come when he looked at the *human* person the coup must come from. An unwelcome question edged into his mind. Had his own physical white father looked like this tired, rather kind-eyed blue-coat chief?

What does it matter? he argued. *I am Comanche in my heart.*

Then why did you find no medicine? mocked an inward voice that sounded like Yellow Wolf's. Why do you risk your life on a raid that will benefit only your worst enemy?

"There's the horse," Yellow Wolf hissed. "The other two in the pen are brown."

Lan located the tall white form. Moonlight surrounded it with a nimbus of silver. It looked like the silver stallion he had seen in his fatigue-induced drowse. "Ha-ii!" he breathed. "A fair bride-price indeed! I think he came from spirit-land and not from over the great waters!"

"He's real enough." Yellow Wolf's tone throbbed with impatience. "Go talk to him in that way you have. When he is quiet, bring him to the gate. I'll have it open and take him. You can get one of the brown horses and we'll be swiftly gone."

The horse-talk gift had always been natural to Lan, like breathing. It had never particularly mattered before if it failed. Now their lives depended on it and this frightened Lan. They waited till the sentry paced by. When he was safely gone, Yellow Wolf slunk towards the corral gate while Lan glided through the rails and towards the white horse. It raised its head. Scenting him, it watched his advance as a seasoned war chief might regard a toddler's war dance. Lan came within ten paces and stopped.

Softly, he spoke. He used that tone, that almost magic horse-talk sound that must have been born in him along with his red hair and blue eyes. The white horse pricked up its ears. It moved in a kind of fear or pleasure, as if Lan's voice stirred something within it that was most pleasant and enticing.

"Hua," Lan crooned, moving closer, his motions soft and flowing as his voice. "Hua, beauty . . ."

It did not matter what he said, even to this horse of the blue-coat soldier which could understand no Comanche. The tone did the work, the rhythm. And these, Lan knew with a sudden thrill of discovery, would be the same anywhere. Even across those broad waters where this horse came from. He, Lan, white-born though he was, had one pride: he could talk to horses anywhere. It made no difference what people accepted or shut him out; that gift was in him.

Close now to the stallion, Lan breathed deep in admiration. "What a prize you are! I'd rather have you than ten wives, white or Comanche. Look, you do not mind that I touch you. You do not mind that I pass my hands along you. You do not mind that I breathe into you my breath."

All the time he talked, Lan had been caressing the horse, smoothing the nervous, trembling legs and body, letting it get his odor and himself absorbing its smell. When he finally took its muzzle in his hands and breathed into its nostrils, he felt his spirit entering the creature, merge with it, forming kinship and a bond between them.

Lan drew back with a sad aching in his heart. He loved this horse, and he had not expected to.

"It is hard," he murmured, coaxing it towards the gate, "to win you and let you be another's. Still, Thunder Waters is a brave chief, and noble. It will be no shame for you to bear him."

Yellow Wolf was waiting tensely with a hackamore. "Here, put this on him," he ordered.

The stallion took the hackamore with only a mild fidget. Lan gave him a good-by pat as Yellow Wolf seized the reins and mounted from the left.

"Why did you do that?" Lan asked indignantly. "Getting on him from the wrong side like that—it's lucky he didn't squeal and throw you!"

"I just wanted to see if you really had the talk-magic," Yellow Wolf jabbed. "Now go back for your horse. I'll hold the gate till you ride it through."

⚔ ⚔ ⚔ *Captured!*

After the white horse, Lan could not care much for any other, but he decided he might as well have something to show for his long hazard. Going back to the pair of browns, he selected the one that looked up without fear as if it found him interesting.

Lan stroked its blazed face and talked to it but he did not want to give it his breath. A quick glance showed that Yellow Wolf, astride the white stallion, waited by the gate. Setting one hand in the brown horse's mane, Lan started to swing on from the right as Comanches almost all did.

The night exploded. Neighing, kicking, struggling, the till now docile horse erupted towards the sky, knocking Lan sideways and almost prostrate. The remaining horse whickered, tearing about the corral with its tail floating straight back. Lan, dizzy, hands skinned, stumbled for the gate as a gun went off and voices sounded from the tents. He could get up behind Yellow Wolf. They could still get away. The gate slammed in Lan's face. He looked up to see Yellow Wolf grinning in the moonlight as he wheeled the white stallion around.

"Didn't your white blood warn you, Bloody Scalp?" came the taunting voice. "Whites mount from the left! That's why I got on the stallion that way. Remember that—if you live to steal any more horses!"

Bitter dust churned back in Lan's eyes and mouth. He stood paralyzed a second. One Comanche leave another like this! But of course! Yellow Wolf had planned it all the time, had urged Lan to steal the brown horse, knowing it would rebel at being mounted from the Indian side. Running feet and the red flare of torches drove everything but the need to escape from Lan's mind. He vaulted the gate.

Shouts and lights were all around him, closing in. Bending low, Lan dodged one man, bowled between two others, and darted for the brush. He might have made it, but something whirred over his head, snapped tight to his arms, yanking them close to his sides. He fell full length in the powdery sand.

Jarred breathless, spitting blood from his mouth, he had time for one clear, terrible thought. Yellow Wolf had not, according to his mind, abandoned a Comanche; he had merely used and discarded an inferior, a white such as the captives who served The People for slaves. Then hands were on Lan, jerking him up.

Voices called things he did not comprehend, but he understood the cuffs and shoves. He shut his face against them. In a way, though no one would ever know, it would be a triumph over Yellow Wolf to act like a Comanche. He would do that—if he could.

One soldier caught his hair, wrenching his head around. Lan gritted his teeth. He was afraid. His knees were water. He prayed silently, desperately, for strength, calling up the strong face of Arrow In His Shield, the gentle eyes of Swift Otter.

Then he heard a new voice. The grip loosened, left his hair. A man not much taller than Lan strode forward. He had a black moustache, but his thick, longish hair was stark white. He held in his hand the other end of the rope that coiled about Lan's body.

"Come along," he said, in the Comanche tongue. "The colonel will want you."

Anger at this man who had caught him and kept him from attaining the shelter of the brush rose stifling in Lan. He said, "It is strange to hear the words of The People in the mouth of a hireling." The man laughed, touching one of Lan's braids.

"No stranger than hearing it from one with hair of this color. You may twine beaver fur in it like a Comanche, but that won't make you one." He loosened the rawhide rope a bit just as someone cried out with surprise over by the corral.

Ah, they'd finally discovered the stallion was gone! As they ran to look, Lan, in spite of his desertion by Yellow Wolf, felt a glow of fierce satisfaction. He peeled back his lips, smiling into his captor's startled face.

"Yes, I stole the white horse. He has been ridden far by now. Your colonel will not see him again."

"But your friend left you to answer for the theft," retorted the man. "You've got nothing to feel happy about!" He started toward the long building.

Head high, keeping pace with the man who spoke Comanche, Lan walked to where the blue-coat chief waited. This man stared at Lan, eyes catching on the unlucky red hair, then he snapped a few orders and went inside. Escorted by two soldiers and the man who had roped him, Lan had to follow.

In the low-ceilinged room, feeling the hostile stares crush in on him like walls, Lan hooded his own gaze. Without seeming to, he studied the roper. Where had he learned Comanche?

Narrow face unlined except for the vertical sun-frown of the plainsman, the man could have been any age under fifty. The moustache, trim and waxed, was the badge of the Mexican dandy. Lan was puzzled by the hair on his head. Strong, young, tough, the strands were not the frazzled corn-husk sort of white one saw on an old man. And though of average height, this man seemed taller than anyone in the room, even the six-foot colonel.

With a wild creature's ability to sense feelings, Lan knew the roper was free and self-owned. He belonged to himself, acted

25

from his own ideas. Surely, right away he would know Lan's weakness, try to break him down before the blue-coat chief who was coming out from behind the table with a lamp. Lan swallowed. He stared the white-haired one in the eye with all his courage.

"Tell the colonel I am glad I stole his horse. His sentries are no good. His corral is no good. If—"

The colonel had come close. Gazing at Lan as if he could not believe what he saw, he held the lamp up higher. Lan felt his eyes contracting to slits in the glare. His chest ached with the breath he had involuntarily sucked in.

"Gor!" said one of the soldiers. The white-haired Mexican spoke rapidly to the colonel who scowled, walked around Lan, and fired questions as fast as a repeating rifle.

"Who are you?" the Mexican asked, translating into Comanche.

"I am called Lan. I am the son of Arrow In His Shield and Swift Otter."

"Ten thousand years would not make you that. The colonel asks how you came to be with Indians."

"Because they are my people!"

The colonel asked a bristling question. "Do you know where your raiding group intends to camp next?" came the translation.

Lan shook his head. The Mexican said something hurriedly, and the colonel, after a savage glance, shrugged and went back to the table. He spoke in a weary tone and signaled. The Mexican nodded at the door.

"Come. You'll stay in the guardhouse till the colonel can think what to do with you."

"Will he not kill me for taking his horse?"

"Not unless you make him. You are fairly caught, my young warrior, so behave with prudence. Try to remember about your real people. It may be that you can be returned to them."

The horrid notion of living among whites broke through

Lan's secrecy. "My parents are dead, the white man and woman!" he blurted. "They were dead of plague when Arrow In His Shield found me."

"It is so? Then perhaps you can be adopted by someone who wants a boy."

"I am Comanche! I will go back to them unless your colonel stakes me to the ground."

"That lies in the future." The Mexican turned to go in another direction. "Enter the guardhouse peaceably and you will be treated well."

They were only a few yards from the squat adobe building. Caught, hemmed in by strangeness, Lan clung to the last familiar thing left him—his language, which the Mexican spoke.

"What is your name?" Lan asked, trying to avoid the time when he would be alone. "How do you know Comanche?"

The man faced about. With a wry smile, he touched his hair. "I am called Blanco for this white," he said. "And I know Comanches as well as their language. They stole me from Durango when I was twelve years old. I saw them kill my family." He walked away softly in his moccasins.

Blindly letting himself be shoved into the evil-smelling, single-celled building, Lan stood in the middle of it.

How the room stank! White man's smell—sweat, tobacco, whiskey. Comanches had an odor, too, but Lan found it familiar and friendly, like the smell of horses and campfires. This soldiers' jail had a sour, bitter, trapped scent, like an animal decayed in a snare.

The guards talked a while. They had barred the door from the outside. One poked in a gourd of water. It smelled almost as bad as the cell, but Lan drank. If he got a chance to escape, he wanted his strength. One of the soldiers strolled off, but the other sat down a little distance from the prison. Lan's head was light and his legs moved under him.

Kicking away a pile of rags and blankets, he sat down. Yel-

27

low Wolf had planned this trip carefully. He would not even have to admit he had taken Lan with him. Swift Otter might think that the spirits had carried Lan off, or that some beast had killed him in his weakened state. Yellow Wolf would give the white stallion to Thunder Waters, marry, and go on many war trails while—

Lan sat up straight, commanding his body that rocked with weariness. *I never got medicine. I'll get no honor from this raid, only captivity or death. But if I live, I'll come back, Yellow Wolf. And no matter what your power, I'll make you ashamed before The People, that before I kill you* . . .

The last thing Lan remembered was repeating this, weaving with fatigue, and the next thing he knew was being roused by a soldier at the door. By his gestures it was plain that Lan was to come with him.

Blinking in the early light, Lan followed the soldier to the long building. His body screamed at every step, he was so stiff, but he tried to move with insouciance. Inside the big room were the colonel, the white-haired Blanco, and an oldish red-cheeked man with grizzled yellow hair. The latter came right up to Lan, thumped his chest, felt his muscles, even set his thumbs in the sides of Lan's jaws to make him open his mouth.

All the rest Lan had endured with what dignity he could muster, but having one's teeth pried at like a traded pony— He bent and sank his teeth into the man's thick, freckled wrist.

The man yelled and jumped back. He started to swing his open palm on Lan's face. But the colonel said something in a stern, clipped voice. Grumbling, the curious man subsided. Lan spat the taste from his mouth. He turned towards Blanco.

"Does that one think I am a horse?"

Blanco grinned. He rolled black tobacco into a cornshuck and held it while he puffed. "He wants to see if you can work hard enough to pay for your keep."

28

"Me? Work for *him*?" Lan would sooner have been the slave of the meanest, dirtiest old squaw.

"He's the sutler," Blanco said. "He supplies the camp with food and necessities."

"That is woman's work! I don't like him." Lan surveyed the man with vast contempt, giving special attention to the broad paunch and short legs. "He may beat me, but I can run away."

Blanco translated this. The colonel puffed out his cheeks. He said a few words to the sutler who returned a torrent of heated speech that made the colonel scowl and cut him off with a sharp, biting word like a dart. The sutler stamped out, giving Lan a murderous side-glance. The colonel sat down at his table. He shook his head. He talked a while to Blanco.

Lan sweated. They seemed to be arguing. What were they saying? To work for that pale, flabby white one, ugh! When it seemed that he had spent his whole life standing in the airless room, Blanco looked around at him.

"Boy," he said, stroking his moustache, "it seems you would not be good help for the sutler. The colonel wishes, then, to send you to a school at Galveston where the good priests would teach you how to be white again."

Panic welled up in Lan. He clenched his hands, fighting it down. In a husky, forced tone he said, "I will find some way to die if I cannot get away. I do not want to be a white! Tell your colonel that!"

Blanco's dark eyes pierced Lan's. "I have told him. I know how you feel. So I have another plan. I am a captain of mustangers, here to talk business with the colonel. Tomorrow I rejoin my band northwest of here at a water hole. We are going to catch and break mounts for the soldiers."

"What has that to do with me?"

"This. You are responsible for the loss of the colonel's fine imported stallion. Now we have long been on the track of a wild white horse called by mustangers The Ghost of the Plains.

Come with me. Work with my band catching wild horses. We are not Comanches, but our way of living would suit you better than that of the towns."

Lan's mouth felt very dry. "For how long would I have to stay with you?"

"Till we catch the Ghost or get back the horse you stole. It may take six months. It may take ten years. But—" Blanco spread his hands. "Either promise yourself to this or go down-river under guard to the white school."

Lan licked his lips. "Why—why should you care what I do?" he asked.

"I have been a captive. And I know it is possible to learn new ways even when the heart is bitter. I learned the ways of the Comanche when my dead brothers' faces floated always before me."

Staring, suddenly positive and wondering why he had not guessed before, Lan cried, "You are Small Man! Thunder Waters' blood brother!"

Blanco's face was inscrutable. "They called me that. But what of you? How will you choose?" Lan looked from Blanco to the colonel's grim expression, but he had already made up his mind.

If he stayed here, he would some day even scores with Yellow Wolf. That he was set upon. Besides, chasing this Ghost— Could he have been the beauty those young mustangers had chased down the creek? Such a hunt shouldn't be dull. Lan crossed his arms.

"I will go with you," he said to Blanco.

⚔ ⚔ ⚔ Captive's Trail

Blanco was not one to idle. Quickly finishing his talk with the blue-coat chief, the mustanger motioned to Lan and led the way out. Dust blowing from the big square struck them in the face. Daylight had not improved the looks of the Fort. Behind the ugly line of adobe buildings were scattered brush-and-mud huts and sagging tents. One group of blue-coats walked in stiff, funny lines under the direction of one who was evidently a kind of war chief from the way he shouted and gestured. On a tall stake fluttered what must be the totem or sign of the whites, a cloth of red and white stripes with a star-studded rectangle in one corner.

What froze Lan to immobility was the sight of the fields beyond the corrals and houses. Those were not squaws hacking at weeds and breaking soil! They were blue-coats. Soldiers!

"What kind of warriors are these?" Lan demanded with a snort. "Their backs will get so bent they can't straighten to fight."

"The Army wants each fort to grow most of its grain. They grow vegetables, too, so they won't get scurvy—that's a bad sickness. Their surgeon told them to do this."

"S-surgeon?" Lan frowned. "What is that?"

It was Blanco's turn to look puzzled. Drawing together the bushy brows which seemed strange after the plucked bare foreheads of the Comanches, the mustanger said, "A surgeon is in a way like a shaman. He tends the sick. Every now and then the forts are visited by one of them who tells the soldiers how to stay healthy."

"If *that* is his advice," sniffed Lan, pointing at the toiling men, "he should be kept away! The People will never be frightened by squaw-warriors who grub in the earth like worms."

Then Blanco said a strange thing. "It is not the blue-coats so much as time that will defeat the Comanches—and not them only, but all the fierce tribes that have held the plains. Apache, Lipan, Kiowa, the northern Sioux and Cheyenne. I may live to see it and you surely will, the day when the Indians will live on lands given as prisons by the great white chief in that place called Washington."

"I have not heard of him. Or this—whatever you call it!"

Blanco smiled grimly. "This chief is head of even the Texans. He commands all these forts, thousands of miles from his lodge. The Comanches have barely started to feel his power. You had best learn white ways, boy. The Indian way is dying."

Lan spat in the dust and scuffed it dry with his moccasin. "That is how I will learn the white ways."

But Blanco's words, as they walked along the corrals, sat on Lan like a bad-luck dream. He recalled snatches of gossip, rumors of parleys which set limits and laws on The People. Some Wasps under Ketumsee had gone to live on a pitiful stretch of land near Clear Fork in the northeast. Each year after the Mexico raids it seemed the warriors grumbled more.

"The Mexicans do not raise mules and horses fast enough," one brave had complained last autumn. "Every fall, like fruit in season, the ranchos lay ready to our hands. We took the best stock and left the poorer beasts to beget our next harvest. But now many ranchos are deserted and what is left isn't worth stealing. We have enough slaves without making that long raid for them."

Listening to this complaint, Lan had privately thought it good sense to move if one had to expect a bloody raid every year when the fall grass grew lush from rain and the Mexico Moon waxed full and yellow.

This seemed a marvel, though, and an outrage to the Comanches, so Lan kept his thoughts to himself. Maybe it was his white blood, treacherously showing him the feelings of tamed, tied-to-the-earth folk. He saw the Comanche view, also. Like corn and berries, honey trees, and the buffalo they hunted after the Mexican raid, The People regarded the settlements as part of their natural supply of good things. That the Mexicans should flee an intolerable situation, cease meekly to garner up animals and plunder, was as incomprehensible to the Comanches as if the buffalo had suddenly stopped bearing flesh and hides.

In spite of this, The People remained the lords of the plains. If the Mexicans were too poor to shear any longer, there were the white settlers.

Glancing at the soldiers humping over their implements, Lan curled his lip. He said to Blanco, "Even if this white chief has droves of these blue-coats, we will beat them. There are many bands of Comanches. We are allies already with the Kiowa; and perhaps you know that about four years ago a great force of Comanches, Osages, Arapahos, Apaches, Kiowas and Cheyennes united to drive out those tame Indians—Cherokees, Seminoles, Delawares and those other eastern tribes who came to our hunting grounds!"

"I have heard of that." Blanco's face wrinkled with amusement. "It is strange you boast of it. For the blue-coat colonel told me that a hundred Sauk and Fox defeated over ten times their number of Plains Indians near the Kansas River. Correct me if I am wrong, but I think that put an end to the great alliance."

Lan simmered. He had not known the defeat was that humiliating. Of course, the news that filtered slowly south was often sketchy and vague. The Southern Comanches had little to do with their northern kindred though they were friendly.

"The Sauk and Fox had rifles," Lan said haughtily. "Our warriors had few firearms, and those weren't much good. Arm both sides with honest weapons and you'd see!"

"Do you think the whites will throw away their guns and fight you with bows and arrows?"

Lan did not answer right off. He looked at the toiling bluecoats with a thrill of dread.

Would Comanches ever come to this? Grubbing in fields, staying on one patch of soil instead of riding free and proud over vast plains, counting wealth in horses instead of land and these ugly houses? Inside a *tipi*, a man was still part of the plains, enclosed by the skins of buffalo. If Comanches ever lived like white men they would not be The People. It was the difference in being a mule burdened till its head drooped and a war horse, prancing to battle. Trying to shake off these sick fancies, Lan spoke jeeringly to Blanco.

"If the whites press on west, the wild horses will go, too. You will have no living."

"The horses will go." Blanco stared past the corrals, the men and animals, as if he saw a vision far off in the brush. "Men like me will vanish. That is why I am almost sad for the Comanches, boy. I know how it will go with them when the buffalo are killed."

"That will never happen!" Those other haunting predictions had a shade of truth, but this was nonsense. "I have seen them like the grass of the prairie, so thick they could hardly graze, and after we took all we needed there were still multitudes."

Blanco's smile had a bitter twist. "Have you seen them after white hunters killed for the Army?"

"There are not as many soldiers as Indians. It should take no more to feed them."

"Ay, boy!" Blanco hooted with laughter. Then his eyes steeled over and his voice shook with anger. "Tell me, what do Comanches do with buffalo?"

Lan pondered this odd question. "Well, what meat we can't eat right away is made into jerky, and of course we eat the tripe, brains, and tongue. Hides are scraped and tanned for *tipis* and clothing and robes. The paunch makes a good water bag. Sinews are used for thread or tying things. Cups are made from hoofs and horns can be drunk from or soaked for bows or used on headdresses."

"And ropes come from the hair. The marrow is eaten and the tallow saved," prompted Blanco.

"Yes. Of all that could be used only the heart is left. That is so the herds will never leave us." Lan eyed Blanco curiously. "Is that not how all people use buffalo?"

Blanco's laugh was between a cry and a curse. "You will see. Listen! I have seen hundreds slaughtered, all the whites could shoot till their arms grew too weary to hold their rifles. And from these hundreds, only the tongue would be gone, or at most, some cuts off the flank."

"You lie!"

"No. It is true. Many whites use the beasts you live on simply for targets—to see how good their aim is."

Lan shuddered at such wickedness. "The Great Spirit will punish them," he blazed. "He will help the Comanches get rid of such wasters of His gifts! Why, that is worse than the Ton-kawas! At least they eat their enemies."

"But you see," explained Blanco with dry humor, "the whites think you are the wicked ones. They are sure the Great Spirit is going to help them kill you. They do not like to see the scalps of their families dangling on your lances."

"They pushed into our hunting grounds," Lan argued.

"And the Mexicans?"

Flushing at the soft question, Lan said, "Well, if—if they were strong enough they'd attack us. Warriors must get horses and war honors. Would you have us be squaws?"

"No. And the whites will use buffalo for targets, Comanches will scalp settlers, and I will hunt mustangs, even the Ghost, while we all pray to the Great Spirit to preserve us as we destroy each other and our own freedom!" Blanco grunted, snapping his tough brown fingers. "People desire their own way and see the ways of others as perversity and madness. Like my daughter. She should wish for marriage and home, but instead wishes only to hunt the mustangs; and she is better at it than most men. How Dios—the Great Spirit—must smile at us all. If He does not weep!"

Pausing by the brush-roofed sheds by the last corral, Blanco gave Lan a rope and an old surcingle. "We'll get you a saddle at our camp," Blanco promised. "For now, catch a horse. I will pay the colonel with a new mustang when we bring a herd back." Lan stayed by the fence, looking over the score of horses, while Blanco, bridle in hand, approached a dish-faced sorrel with a slanting rump and sparse tail. The animal pricked up his ears and shifted around, keeping his face towards Blanco.

"This is the best—not the fastest, but the most enduring, of the horses we took last year," Blanco called over his shoulder. "Wicked he is, till mounted."

I could talk him to gentleness, Lan thought, but kept still. He hoped the sorrel did give Blanco a bad time. Ignoring a pair of blue-coats who were gesturing at him and making scalping motions while they laughed and made fun, Lan studied the mounts.

His horse-loving Comanche eye singled out almost automatically a clean-legged dun, the color called *maana* by The People. Leaving the surcingle on the fence, Lan moved close to the *maana*, coming from behind on his right. He would loop the rope over its neck and—

A flash of neat black hoofs, whoops of laughter from the pair of soldiers made him pause.

"*Hola!*" Blanco called. "You'll get kicked that way. Go along his left."

Ears burning, Lan worked around to the *maana's* other side. How, after being captured because he got on a white man's horse Indian fashion, could he have forgotten? Weird it was and unnatural, but these horses were trained to it. Arrow In His Shield had always said, "To make a mistake once is a good way to learn. To make it twice is a fool's trick."

Speaking softly to the horse, Lan held it with his voice while he worked the loop over its head. It paced restlessly but did not dodge or resist. Lan brought him out the gate and hitched him. Blanco, who was saddling the resentful sorrel, pointed to the gear hanging in the shed. "Take one of the bridles. The colonel said he could spare it."

Lan eyed the contrivance with its metal bar. Used to the simple plaited hair or hide bridle of the Comanches, he thought this a cruel-looking thing. Blanco noticed his hesitation.

"Oh, that's right, you've never used a bit. You'll need one on that horse; he's used to them. Just stick it in his mouth."

Gingerly, Lan obeyed. The metal clicked on the *maana's* big squarish teeth and he seemed to chew at it, but once Lan had the strap behind the ears and the band around the neck fastened as Blanco's was, the horse quit fidgeting. The buckle on the band and the surcingle gave Lan a little trouble, but by observing Blanco he managed. Remembering his earlier humiliation, Lan vaulted onto the horse from the left after unhitching from the fence. He fastened the short rope so it would not drag or get in the *maana's* way and turned in time to see the scrubby-looking sorrel wrench his head around, diving for Blanco with eager teeth as the mustanger started to mount.

Quick as thought, Blanco smacked the side of his rigid hand across the sorrel's nose. It squealed and reared. Blanco, though his hand must have stung furiously from striking the thinly covered bone, swung to the saddle. As if by strong medicine, the sorrel changed its behavior.

Responding docilely to bridle and knee pressure, it moved from the corral. A mule, branded with the symbol U S, ran along the corral, splitting the air with brays, which, though raucous, held an unmistakable note of distress. Blanco jerked his head at him.

"That's old Pelón, Baldy. He got away once and ran with mustangs. He'd give his ears to come with us."

One of the soldiers shouted something to Blanco. When Blanco, frowning, shook his head, the soldier spat out a wad of tobacco that struck the *maana's* rump. Quieting the horse, Lan glared over his shoulder.

"You cannot expect them to love you," Blanco said.

"They are dogs!" Lan burst out. "Their chief gave judgment and they murmur against it."

Blanco gave a dry laugh. "Don't try to tell me Comanches always support their chiefs. I've lived with you, remember!"

"Then you know that when a chief, either war or civil, is not trusted, he ceases to be one. It is The People's belief that he is worthy that makes him chief in the first place."

"It is a good way," Blanco assented, to Lan's surprise. "But it wouldn't work with the whites. Most of them think they know better than their leaders. They wouldn't follow him if they didn't have to. Strong rules are made. Blue-coat soldiers can be shot if they dispute orders and a judge, or civil chief, can sentence men to death or prison for breaking laws."

"A crazy people! They have chiefs they do not trust and yet kill men for disobeying them?"

"It is different." Blanco's furrowed brow showed that he searched for a way to explain. "Comanches respect the *man* who is their chief. Whites respect the law though possibly not the man who enforces it. And they must obey their war chief no matter what they think of him."

"Hai!" was all Lan could say. Why, among The People, a war chief who was disliked or cowardly or stingy, could not even get enough warriors to go with him to make a raid. That was plainly the only way to get rid of bad leaders—not follow them. He blurted, "Why should the blue-coat chiefs try to be good leaders if they must be followed anyway?"

"Some of them don't. Most do their best for the simple reason that they like to be well thought of, just as most Comanches behave so as to have good standing among The People. But you see, white soldiers must be ruled differently than warriors. Among you, all able-bodied men are warriors. That is how you get honor and possessions and a name. But whites can do this by being merchants or doctors, farmers, ranchers, government chiefs, teachers—oh, many things. Only a few whites are soldiers. These serve for pay, as steady work, not for their independent glory and profit. Except for their high chiefs, soldiers are not especially honored among the whites. Many positions are ranked higher."

Was Blanco joking? Scanning him, Lan decided he spoke truth. "We will beat them, then." Lan spoke with scornful confidence. "We will drive these reluctant soldiers with their merchants and farmers off our lands forever, back into the sea. Back to where the blue-coat chief's horse came from, across the great water."

"If there were only two whites for each Indian, or even only ten, this might be. But they are countless, and they push across the Mississippi like flood waters spilling. Have you not heard how they drove the Cherokees and other southeastern Indians west along the Trail of Tears? Those Indians now cramp you

Plains tribes, but the whites sweep on. Their trappers have long been in the mountains, their merchants travel to Santa Fe and Taos, the wagons roll still to the gold in California. In fifty years they will have covered this country as honey saturates a comb."

"I see you give yourself time enough to die before all this is completed."

Blanco shrugged. "I am what I am. You and the young men must learn a different life."

"That is how older men always talk," Lan retorted. "They like to think the world will not last beyond them."

"Mine will not."

They rode in silence till the sun cast their shadows straight beneath them. Blanco dismounted and Lan was glad to join him. They sipped water from the Army canteen Blanco carried and he shared a pouch of ground corn mixed with a sweetening that Blanco said was brown sugar.

"We use *pinole* almost as Comanches use pemmican," the mustanger said. "Promise your stomach a better meal tonight. There should be fresh meat in camp."

Back on the *maana*, weak from his long vigil and the hectic night and day since then, Lan had a hard time staying awake. He began to think it might be nice to have a peaked hat like Blanco's to shut out the sun. As evening lengthened and a cool breeze sprang up, Lan felt better. When they struck the river bed, he peered intently ahead, straining for his first glimpse of the camp.

They rode around a slope and started down the valley that narrowed on the dry river. Lan's eyes picked up the outline of the pen and the scattering of men and horses. Blanco pointed.

"There it is." A touch of pride enriched his voice. "See, we have repaired the walls and put up a new cross. This is the Corral of the Blessed Saint James."

40

⚑ ⚑ ⚑ *The Corral of the Blessed Saint James*

Muscles tense, throat dry, Lan did not puzzle over the outlandish name. He realized for the first time that he was going among people who feared and hated Comanches—and with reason. Many, if not all the mustangers, would have scores to settle for kidnapped or murdered families, stolen goods and horses.

Comanches tested prisoners, and killed the cowards. Lan expected no better treatment now. Had not Blanco seen his people killed, endured taunts and pain as a slave till he became Thunder Waters' blood brother? Maybe his taking Lan was an elaborate form of revenge for what he had suffered. Lan set his jaw. He sat erect as befitted one of The People and the son of Arrow In His Shield, keeping level with Blanco as they neared the camp.

"*Eeee-i-yaaooou!*"

As the jubilant shout shrilled up the valley, two figures streaked for horses, hurtled astride, and bore down on the newcomers. Lan had seen them before—the rangy claybank, the trim black, and their riders. The girl and boy he had seen chasing the stallion down the river bed!

The red ribbon still swept back the girl's black hair. A side glance at Blanco convinced Lan this was the daughter he had spoken of with mingled pride and misgiving. Pride and love wiped out every other feeling in the mustanger's face. He reined up, calling a greeting in Spanish.

One on either side, the pair swept down on Blanco. The girl leaned out of her brass-stirrupped saddle to kiss him and the boy bowed his dark head low over Blanco's hand. The horses curvetted but seemed resigned to these demonstrations.

Lan, outside the warm group, felt a rush of loneliness—for his mother, for his father whose hand he could never touch again—before he turned grimly away.

What carrying-on! Why, no Comanche would behave like this! One would have thought Blanco had been gone ten years instead of a few days. Also, the way the young squaw behaved was a scandal. He heard their laughing talk cease and faced around to meet dawning hostility in the boy's eyes, curiosity in the girl's. Blanco spoke to them in Spanish before he explained to Lan.

"This is my daughter Marina, and my godson, Miguel. Miguel will show you where to eat and sleep. Remember, I have your word you will not escape."

"How could I forget?" Lan asked bitterly. He gave the boy —what was a godson?—an answering glare and drew his *maana* off to a slight distance.

Not that he was jealous of these three. To show one's feelings like that and in the open, before a prisoner? Still—

The girl's voice, soft and rippling like the fresh mountain brooks, thrummed in his ears. He was sure she was asking about him. Blanco answered briefly, and cut Miguel off short when the boy started to growl some protest.

It seemed that Blanco, after all, did rule these children, for Miguel subsided though he continued to cast challenging looks at Lan when Blanco was not watching. Lan pretended to ignore him and surveyed the camp as they approached it.

The corral, spiral in form, spread its brushy walls above the ford by the water hole. It fronted on the south, its wings spreading widely from the gate so that many horses could enter the passageway. If the wind was from the south they would scarcely be able to see their prison till they were headed into it, for the dust they raised would fly on in front of them. The wings were made completely of brush, stacked high and wide so that the horses could neither see through nor jump them. The corral employed scantily-available timber for support stakes which held up piled limbs and brush. So long as the walls looked solid, the mustangs would believe they were. Comanches, when after a herd instead of individual horses, used similar catch pens.

On the opposite bank, situated carelessly along the slope, were a few brush shelters, open on all sides, a two-wheeled cart, and yes—a *tipi!* Blanco, leaving his animated talk with his daughter for a moment, pointed at the whitened hide cone and grinned.

"I got it for Marina. A good *tipi* is far better than most settlers' houses and certainly is the best thing for us travelers."

Twilight picked up the gleam of the small cook-fires dotting the camp. Men lounged near them or were busy with cooking. The horses and mules grazed at will around the valley and Lan heard the tinkle of bells as some of the horses moved. Perhaps the bells kept the other animals from straying.

As they rode into camp, most of the men jumped up, pressing around Blanco with greetings and questions. They noticed Lan with varying reactions, but suspicion and hate were the common ones. Lan fixed his eyes above their heads and stared off at the darkening plains. From the way Blanco had acted he might not let his men torture or maim Lan, but there was bound to be some trouble and some men who would do what they could to hurt him. A hand with nails like talons clamped on Lan's knee.

He looked down. From the blur of strange faces, one came into focus, burned into his mind with odd, yellow eyes. Stringy yellow hair hung down the man's shoulders, touching a buckskin shirt that had once been fine and soft but was now stiff with grease and filth for all its bead and concho trim. In one ear was a fiery blue gem. Skin, burned red-brown, showed a rim of white where the shirt opened.

Roaring in the barbarous tongue of the whites, this man laughed hugely, grabbed Lan's arm, and had wrenched him half to the ground when Blanco rapped out an order.

The blond one paused. Then, with a wink around at the men, he gave Lan another tug.

This time Blanco did not speak. He brought round his braided four-strand rawhide rope, almost half-an-inch thick, and slammed its coiled length into the man's face.

Fighting free of the strands, stumbling back, the man snarled. His hand snaked into his shirt. For a second a leather scabbard showed before it fell back into its concealment and a fourteen-inch blade flashed in the firelight, its curved point sharply ground on both sides so that besides the long front of the blade there was a thirsty two-and-a-half-inch edge on the back. Crouching, the man took a step towards Blanco.

Before anyone could move, the girl rode by the blond, kicking the knife from his hand. He yelled with pain, but bent for his weapon.

"Inglés!" Blanco was off his horse, gripping the rebel's arm. Foot planted on the knife, Blanco cut at the man with words that cracked like whips. The other mustangers had come close. They watched the blond with every emotion but that of liking on their wild faces.

Abruptly, Blanco released the red-faced man. The blond scooped up his knife, eyed Blanco, and then, wiping the dust from the wicked blade, sheathed it in the scabbard he wore suspended from a leather thong about his neck. Turning sullenly, he moved over to a fire, walking so that the men had to get out of his way.

Blanco walked up to his daughter, swung her down from her horse. Pride vibrated in his voice, though he was plainly chiding her for the mad risk. He had his hands full with this one, Lan thought. She had spirit, valor even. But these were more attributes for warriors than women. Plainly Miguel thought so, too, for he frowned at Marina and said something that made her show her tongue and toss her head.

Lan slid down from the *maana*. The steady riding close upon his medicine fast had weakened him so that his head reeled. He staggered, caught his horse's mane.

"Have you fever?" Blanco asked.

Lan shook the fuzziness from his head. "My ankle turned." Fumbling with the unfamiliar bit, he mercifully got the bridle off before Marina could help as she had obviously started to. Pushy squaw! Lan, following Blanco's example, tossed the surcingle and bridle across a junco bush to dry.

"We will get some food in you," Blanco said. "That will keep your ankle from turning." He added softly, "The blond one called Inglés hates Indians. Keep from his path. I have commanded him but he has violent blood."

"Do not your men obey you?"

"If he attacks you, I will punish him, but will that heal your death wound? Have a care and save us all trouble." Blanco's smoldering eyes with their touch of flame in the darkness bored into him. "Listen well! It is my order that you be left in peace. But these are hard men, a hard life. Do as you're told and keep a soft tongue."

He did not add, as he must have felt like doing, that a Comanche captive would already have been tasting hurts designed to gauge his bravery and potential value to the tribe. Those who failed this savage test died, and horribly. Lan had never been able to watch. He had managed to be off hunting when new captives came.

But at least Comanche captives had no choice of behavior. Lan did not know what to do, left relatively free as he was. No one shoved him here or kicked him there. Neither did they wait on him.

Blanco had gone to the fire nearest the cart. Marina was filling a bowl for him from the big iron kettle, while Miguel rolled black tobacco into a cornshuck and lit it for his godfather. The boy made a second cigarette for an old man leaning against one of the huge cart wheels, and lastly, one for himself.

The smell of meat twisted through Lan's straining nostrils into his stomach. He found himself edging towards the kettle as if drawn by a current. When no one objected, or even seemed to notice him, he reached in with his fingers and pulled out a piece of meat.

Dripping with a spiced red gravy, steaming hot to his tongue and fingers, it was so good he wolfed it down and started to fish out a nice-looking hunk when Marina jumped up.

Scolding away at him, she got a wooden bowl from the cart, ladled it full of meat and gravy. This she handed him along with a horn spoon. Lan, flushing, retired to the shadows, but he relished the food to the last savory speck. He could handle the spoon without trouble; Swift Otter had several made from buffalo horn and bone. The meat, under all its disguise of seasonings, had the rank taste of wild pig meat.

Hunger satisfied, Lan was content to stay out of the light and watch these people he would live among. The men had waited for Blanco to eat. As he finished, they wandered over in twos and threes, squatting around to talk.

Evidently they were pleased with the news from the Fort, for they laughed and gestured towards the corral, speaking in boastful or hopeful tones. After a while the men strolled off, breaking into groups that played cards, rolled dice, or simply talked and smoked. One young man with slanting eyes and high cheekbones leaned against a pile of saddles and played on a stringed instrument. He sang, and his listeners came in at the chorus, ululating, clapping.

Like coyotes, Lan thought. He grinned as off in the night a coyote answered, and several more joined in. The mustangers laughed and sang. "*Ay-ay-ay-ay* . . ." and Coyote answered from the small hills, "*Yi-yi-yi-yi* . . ."

Lan realized with astonishment that Comanches might have done much the same thing. Coyote often warned of danger, and a few old Comanches could still talk the coyote language. Once a little boy had been lost and reared by coyotes. When he came back to the tribe, he taught the Indians how to speak with Coyote. Coyote was mischievous and always played tricks, but he was close kin to Wolf, the good and great benefactor of man. Therefore, Comanches respected Coyote and did not eat him or kill him without good reason.

From the singers, Lan glanced around at the other men. Except for Inglés, they all looked Mexican. They were mostly young, though Miguel was the only boy who looked under twenty. They all wore leather trousers, slit up one calf to reveal white underpants. These slits plainly were fastened for riding. There all similarity ceased. Shirts were everything from buckskin to frilled white, some wore leather vests and jackets, others had a blanket over one shoulder. Footwear ranged from moccasins to heeled boots which might be rough hide or beautifully inlaid and stitched leather. Together, the mustangers numbered twelve. Lan did not count himself or the squaw, Marina.

Inglés, seemingly unaware that Lan existed, was playing cards with fierce concentration. The gem in his ear flashed blue and green and yellow, half-hidden by the lank coarse hair that fell across it. The three men playing with Inglés joked and laughed, but the white man seemed conscious only of the colored rectangles. Lan marveled at the difference in white men.

The colonel at the Fort was like a shaggy, majestic buffalo bull, gentle unless roused. The sutler was a pig. But this blond had the smooth motions, tawny color, and cruel eyes of a mountain lion. He was strong and fast and he hated Indians. With a prickle at the back of his neck, Lan got up and moved to the other side of the cart. From there he could see Miguel throwing his rope.

Grave and intent as if his life depended on it, Miguel coiled and tossed the rawhide. He was using for his target a tall spire of prickly-pear cactus, picking off the flat leaves one at a time. In this flickering light, to get the aimed-for leaf each time was wonderful.

Lan, a good roper even among The People who excelled at it, felt grudging admiration. Could he do that? Duplicate the deft turn of wrist that flipped the rope just so? Leaning forward to study the young mustanger's technique, Lan jumped at the soft cackle behind him.

"So a Comanche pup can admire the skill of Miguel la Changa?" The question was in Comanche! Whirling, Lan stared into the wrinkled face of the old man who still hunched against the cart, strands of rawhide momentarily loose in his hands. His streaked gray hair was bound back with a beaded leather band and his grin showed only three scraggly teeth, but his eyes were clear and black.

"Where did you learn the tongue of The People?" Lan asked.

"I learned it along with how to dodge kicks and blows and wait my chance." Gazing back in time, the old man rubbed his wattled neck. He laughed in a dry, hacking way that chilled Lan's blood. "I was a slave among the Honey-Eaters for ten years. I made them many fine ropes. Had it not been for this they would have killed speedily an older man like me. Then one Feast of the Green Corn I took my strongest, thickest rope, woven from the chief's favorite horse's tail. With it I strangled the chief, my master, and got away. Five years ago."

Lan had stiffened during this story. Honey-Eaters was another name for his tribe, the Wasps. Of course, there were many scattered groups of them. But this crazed-acting old man had a chief's death on his hands. He deserved death. Trained fingers went back to plaiting rawhide.

"Blanco says you are white, not truly Comanche. So I will not strangle you tonight with one of my ropes. You shall live unless Inglés kills you, and I will teach you a human language instead of that turkey-gobbling."

"I will not learn that woman's tongue," Lan retorted. "It is not fit for warriors though it is suitable for serenading coyotes."

Blanco had stepped up before Lan knew he was close. White hair shining in the ruddy light, the mustanger chief rolled a cigarette, lit and handed it to the old ropemaker, who took a puff, bowed his head in thanks, and then fixed his sharp look on Lan.

"The Spanish was fit for the great *conquistadores* who took away the empire of the Aztecs and could have taken your accursed lands, too, had they been worth anything."

Lan shrugged. "I do not know those names, what you talk about." Blanco, smothering a grin, spoke peaceably.

"It is well, boy, to understand the speech of those you live among. Otherwise you are like an animal that must be driven or coaxed, but cannot follow only words. Do not make us treat you like a balky mule. Only Javier and I speak Comanche and we will not always be near."

It seemed treason to use the language of his captors but,

resentfully, Lan knew Blanco was right. Already he had burned to know what was being said among the mustangers, especially since he was sure most of it concerned him. He looked sullenly at Blanco.

"You want me to forget The People. You would make my ears deaf to their language."

"I would close your ears to nothing—only open them to more." Blanco's voice hardened with a touch of that iron he had shown Inglés. "When you are not busy, you will sit evenings and other times with Javier. He will teach you Spanish."

"I—"

Blanco cut in like a slicing tomahawk. "Do as you are told or I send you to the Fort and from there you go to the Galveston school. It is one to me. I have no time for burros."

A hot, sick trembling spreading from his stomach to his legs, Lan clenched his hands, gritting his teeth together. He could not escape it any longer; he was a slave. Like any captive dragged north from Mexico to drudge among The People! He, the only son of Arrow In His Shield, that proud chief and warrior!

These mustangers would not torture him, cut him with knives or pierce him with arrows. They would not test his courage, they did not care if he had any. They would simply treat him like a servant, make him bend his tongue to theirs, and any time he rebelled, Blanco would threaten him with that unthinkable school far away where there were no Comanches and no respectable horses. If he had only died in the blue-coat chief's corral! When he got back to Yellow Wolf—

The image of his false comrade's jeering face rose before Lan. A fresh charge of anger coursed through him. Yes, there was Yellow Wolf to be settled with. Lan swallowed.

Well! Then he would learn what he had to and serve out the term of his promise to Blanco. And what would be the fury and shame of Yellow Wolf when he came face to face again with the boy he had tricked and delivered to the whites! Sinking down by Javier, Lan said gruffly, "I will learn."

A smile stirred the spiders' webs of wrinkles about the old eyes and mouth. One hand, tough and gnarled as an aged eagle's, touched Lan on the bare ankle.

"I will teach you the names of some things tonight, lad, and how the men are called. Repeat after me. Fire is *fuego*, rope, *reata*. Man is *hombre*, woman, *mujer*."

Lan repeated these words, and the others Javier pronounced, fixing his attention on them to learn as quickly as possible since he had to. Javier nodded approvingly.

"When you make the 'v' sound, you must learn to do it without holding your lips together as the Comanches do. Otherwise you do well. Now I will name the men. That one singing is Chon. He is our best shot and the only thing he loves better than his rifle is his guitar. The men playing with Inglés are Lázaro, Cruz, and Felipe, the Sauz brothers. See, they trim their moustaches alike. Lázaro is thin, Cruz short, and Felipe is both thin and short."

On through the men Javier went, giving each one a trait or characteristic so that Lan could tell them apart more easily. At length Javier nodded to the boy roper who was coiling his *reata* and walking over to Blanco and Marina.

"Miguel is called 'la Changa' which means the Monkey, because he can swing himself by his rope as a monkey swings by his tail." When Lan frowned in puzzlement, Javier laughed.

"That's right, you don't know what monkeys are. Well, they are small animals that get around in trees as agilely as squirrels, but they look much like tiny men with hair and tails. There aren't any trees around here big enough for Miguel to show off on, but you have seen he is marvelous with his rope."

Lan had to nod agreement, just as Miguel came up. He

51

yanked two blankets out of the cart, tossed one carelessly to Lan, and spoke to Javier, who translated. "It is time to rest. You will sleep between Miguel and the cart."

Lan was too tired to care if he had to sleep by his worst enemy—and that honor was reserved for Yellow Wolf. Spreading out the tightly-woven black, brown, and white blanket, Lan folded half of it over him. Before he had gouged out a comfortable place for his shoulder in the hard soil, he was asleep.

⚔ ⚔ ⚔ Wrestle with the Monkey

Lan woke to a peculiar, unpleasant smell. Was Swift Otter brewing a medicinal tea he would have to drink? Raising himself on one elbow, he glanced about cautiously. His heart plummeted as he realized he was far from his mother's *tipi*. About him was the morning bustle of all camps. Lan was out of his blanket and rolling it up in almost one motion. He stowed it in the cart and came to the fire where Javier seared meat over an open flame, holding it on a stick.

"*Buenos días,*" said the old man. "That means good morning. You slept well?"

There was no honor in quibbling with old men. Lan bit back a sarcastic reply. "Well enough."

"Weariness makes a soft bed and hunger the best sauce. Enjoy your breakfast." The ex-captive tossed Lan the long flap of juicy meat. "I was going to tickle your nose with this in a minute if you hadn't waked. Blanco and the young ones have already eaten. They have gone to see to one of the horses that has a bad saddle-sore."

Methodically, Javier poured dirt on the fire and thrust his blanket in the cart. Lan noticed that he limped very badly, seeming able to little more than drag his right leg. He turned.

Lan glanced quickly away. The old ropemaker gave his croaking laugh.

"You wonder what happened? It was not a wild horse, nor yet a fall. Till I had forty-five years, I walked like any proud man, even among the Comanches. Too proudly, the chief, my master, thought. He feared I would run away and he would lose my ropes. So he cut the tendons at the back of my knee." That rustling cackle sounded again. "Still, I got away. Though I dragged myself over the Staked Plains like a crushed beetle. Blanco found me where I had fallen sick at a dry water hole. He cared for me, expecting nothing, and it has been pride, though I must walk crooked to my coffin, to make his band the finest, strongest ropes in all this country."

Lan had known vaguely that some warriors were cruel to their slaves just as he knew that some had come to love their captives and made them blood brothers, bestowing their sisters or daughters on them in marriage. Many a Comanche warrior was in truth a Mexican or white who could not have been forced to leave The People. But it did not help to think of them while Javier limped about tidying the camp. Lan got up, still chewing the half-raw meat, and helped. It was squaw work but plainly Marina could not manage for the whole camp and seemed to have no intention of minding even her family's needs.

A gust of the strong acrid smell that had waked him blew into Lan's nostrils. He looked around, frowning. "What is that bad smell?"

"Bad smell?" Javier seemed about to take offence. Then his nose wrinkling, too, he glanced at the last eater, who happened to be Inglés, and grinned. "Ay, if Inglés could only understand you! That smell is his coffee."

"Cof-fee?" Lan tried the unfamiliar word. "A medicine?"

Javier whooped with pleasure. "It is a drink most Texans cannot live without. They must have it mornings or they are meaner than black fighting bulls. Inglés carries his sealed in a tin box wrapped in oiled cloth inside oiled hide. If we have to ford deep water, he carries it above his head along with his rifle. When his supply gets low, he makes for the nearest settlement to buy more, even if it is two hundred miles away and we are about to pen a fine herd."

Lan gaped. He could not believe a drink could have such power on a man, though when he stopped to think of it, he recalled a few braves who had found some kind of "wild water" in Mexico and become so addicted to it that they would sell anything they owned for a jug. The People did make a popular drink from corn which was sweetened with mesquite, but it did not make men foolish as did the "wild water" which the Comancheros called *mescal*.

"Have you tasted this cof-fee?" Lan asked.

Javier made a face. "It is not half so good as chocolate. Some of our men like it and buy it when they have money, but Inglés insists on his. I think he would go without meat first."

"He is crazy."

"Without doubt."

"Why does Blanco trouble with him? The blond even attacked him last night."

Scooping up a handful of parched corn which must have been hard to chew with as few teeth as he had, Javier squinted thoughtfully at Lan. "Blanco is the captain. He also is my friend. Why he tolerates Inglés is none of my business, or yours."

"But—"

"Blanco feels he owes Inglés gratitude for a favor. One might better wonder why the captain bothers with you. 'El que no quiere ruido que no críe cochinos.' That means, boy, he who doesn't like noise shouldn't raise hogs—and that means, live and let live!"

Rolling a cigarette, Javier gobbled down his corn in a way

that made Lan sure the old fellow must have a craw like a turkey to digest bone and unchewed food. Beyond them, Inglés downed a final steaming tin cup of the coffee he poured from a small kettle. Rising, the lion showed in the man as he stretched and faced the sun. Either he was disliked or he ate alone to safeguard his precious, stinking coffee. Perhaps it had some magic property; it smelled bad enough. What a shaman could not do with just that odor!

Inglés kicked dirt on the fire, and left it smoldering while he tucked the small kettle and a carefully wrapped bundle into the cart. He seemed unable to see Lan and did not speak to Javier, or to anyone else as he moved off towards the horses.

"He is like that," Javier murmured. "No one calls to him unless he shows he is in the mood. His temper will kill him someday, split him wide open."

"No loss," Lan snorted.

Javier got out his leather and started to work. "Go see if Blanco wants you. They may hunt meat today, for we are almost out. It spoils fast in this weather."

"You mean we do not go at once after mustangs?" Lan's dismayed tone brought a disapproving stare from Javier.

"You think the Ghost should be chased down immediately so you may have your freedom? Well, let me tell you that we earn our livings from this and must catch two hundred horses for the Army, not that white stallion alone. Now go!"

Smarting, Lan moved down the valley to the water hole where most of the men were catching their horses. He sighted Blanco, Marina, and Miguel la Changa over by a deep-chested, stocky little bay. Ugly running sores covered its back. Lan winced at them though he had seen cruelly lacerated backs on Comanche horses, too. Arrow In His Shield had never ridden or permitted Lan to ride a horse with a raw back.

A shamefaced man whom Javier had identified last night as Mateo Rodriguez, an ex-lancer in the Mexican army, stood on shifting feet as Blanco addressed him in stinging, short words.

Marina, with gentle fingers, rubbed a strong-smelling grease over the sores. She handed the remaining stuff in its little box to Mateo, along with some comments that dyed his face scarlet. He pulled the bridle off the horse and let it wander off, cropping at the curly mesquite grass. Marina blew a curl from in front of her nose, wiping her hands on her leather skirt-trousers. These, falling below the calf, seemed a compromise between skirts and pants, for though slit up the center and stitched, they were full as a skirt and must have been cumbersome. A yellow ribbon held back her hair today and a golden cross showed at her throat. Discovering Lan, she smiled.

"*Buenos días.*"

Miguel scowled at this. As much to annoy him as practice his Spanish, Lan said "*Buenos días.*" Marina clapped her hands. Blanco gave Lan a quizzical look.

"So you learn. That is good. I hope you already know that a horse as galled as that bay should be turned out for graze till it's healed."

"My father taught me that. Also we made a salve of jimson weed that was helpful."

Blanco nodded. "That is a cure. But I like grease best and we had this fresh from the brush-hog we ate yesterday. That meat's all gone. We must go today and hunt down enough game to feed us while we chase the wild ones."

"Is there a herd close?" Lan asked hopefully.

"Mustangs always graze close to their customary watering spot. Usually their range is not over twenty miles. A herd of at least fifty have been drinking here, but of course when we camped, they circled off. After we have laid up a meat supply, we'll locate them and try to walk them back here. Is this all new to you? I thought Comanches caught horses in corrals, though they prefer to steal them."

"Of course," said Lan. "That counts as honor! Sometimes The

People use corrals but usually if we want mustangs, we catch them after they have drunk and are weighted down, or in the full grass time when they get fat. I have never helped pen a herd."

"You will learn." Blanco's eyes swept over Lan who was still dressed in the breech clout and moccasins he had worn on his medicine search. "That garb won't do for tearing through the brush. Come. Some of Miguel's clothes will fit you."

Lan held back. He would rather be scratched bloody than wear that unfriendly boy's things. "I'll be all right."

"Yes, after you dress in trousers and have something over your arms." Blanco strode off in a way that allowed no argument.

At the cart, Blanco pulled out a buffalo hide bag, rather like those used by Comanches to hold their finest clothes. After some rummaging he produced tight leather trousers, a vest, and a red shirt. "The shirt and vest are mine and may be a little loose, but you are skinnier even than Miguel, so the pants should be no problem."

Resignedly, Lan got into the clothes. Javier, who had watched, grinning, trilled a surprised whistle. "When your eyebrows grow out no one would guess you ever saw the inside of a Comanche *tipi!*" Lan drew himself up.

"It is more than outward looks that makes one of The People."

"True," said Javier dryly. "It takes the blood you don't have." He bent over his work. Lan stalked away, following Blanco to the corral for his bridle. An old but serviceable saddle had been found for him, and he quickly had the *maana* ready to go, talking to it softly.

"I will call you Friend," he said, touching it on legs and withers, throat, and rump, letting it feel his breath. "You may be my only one for long and long. I will take care of you and you will carry me well. This is good?" Friend looked at him

58

with almost human comprehension. Lan smiled and stroked him.

Arrow In His Shield had said often, *"Be sure of two choices, your horse and your wife."* Lan was in no hurry for a wife, but he agreed positively about the horse. He also resolved to make one of the Comanche bridles with merely a nose loop instead of the metal bit.

Blanco had saddled a new horse this morning. As he rode up, Lan mounted, remembering to swing on from the left. He was scarcely finding the hide-covered stirrups with his feet when Friend skittered. Gaining control, Lan glared at the twin dust-devils that had shot past him on either side. Those two fool children! Marina was his age, perhaps, and Miguel older, but they behaved like *tuinvp,* boys not yet in adolescence. Lan was glad that they rode on together and left him with time to question Blanco.

"The white Ghost—is he with this herd that waters here?"

"No. He leads another group or *manada* which we tried to pen last week. He scattered them and got away. Miguel and Marina saw and chased him while I was gone, but he scaled the arroyo banks and escaped." Blanco laughed, glancing with amused pride at the pair ahead. "They were disappointed, I can tell you! Had they caught the Ghost you could have heard them shouting as far as Monterrey. By now he will have collected his mares and headed for another place."

"I hope we catch him soon," Lan said, more to himself than aloud.

He jumped at Blanco's dry chuckle. "I'll wager you do. But don't hold your breath till the ropes fall on him. I have chased him for four seasons, and so have other mustangers."

"Perhaps we'll have luck."

"Perhaps the next norther will rain palominos."

Biting his lip, Lan silently resolved never to use his horse-talk for the benefit of these mustangers. They could make him wear these clothes, speak Spanish, and work, but that gift was his to employ or hide. He would hide it. Blanco's voice roused him from brooding.

"We'll scatter into threes. That rope on your saddle is not too good but perhaps you can catch a slow brush-hog with it. I'll send my children back to stay with you."

Lan had to know. "Miguel—is he your real son? I do not understand what you call him."

"Godson? No, you wouldn't. Well, I was in the church when he was baptized. You won't understand that, either, but it is very solemn, when babies are given a name and the Great Spirit is invoked for them. His real parents, distant cousins of mine, asked me to be his godfather. That is, I am responsible for him if anything happens to them, and I must help him in all ways I can." When Lan still frowned, Blanco clapped his saddle with desperate inspiration. "It is nearest to what your Comanches called *tawk*—the mother's father who teaches his grandson the use of weapons and tribal lore and other useful things."

Lan had a fair idea of the relationship now. It made sense. Swift Otter had never scolded him herself. She had called in her sister who was certainly happy to do it. Few Comanches punished their children and when it was absolutely necessary they got a relative or friend to do it. Blanco rode up by Marina and Miguel, spoke, and rode on to join one of the scattering groups of mustangers who were going off in all directions. Marina waited, but Miguel looped his rangy claybank, galloped past Lan, and then swooped back, swatting Friend over the ears as he did so.

"*Ándale!*" Lan knew that word. It meant hurry, which Friend was doing. Only Lan's lifetime on horseback saved him an ignominious tumble. He righted himself quickly, though, and pretended nothing had happened.

That made Miguel glower, as Lan had intended it should.

They were beside Marina in a minute. It was a bright morning with fresh tangy smells of *huajillo*, salt cedar, and sage in the air. Lan could almost feel his blood run light and happy in his veins. At least, in spite of this Miguel la Changa, he was still with horses, roaming the plains. That was inexpressibly better than being shut up with white boys in some terrible school.

Gradually, though, the certainty that Miguel and Marina were discussing him burned into Lan's consciousness. Punctuated by glances at him, Marina's words sounded defensive while Miguel's were contemptuous.

A burn spread from Lan's ears all over him. He gripped the greasy reins till his fingers ached. Did this Mexican, this "peeled-one" actually think that he, a Comanche, was afraid?

He met Miguel's next stare with a haughty one of his own. Miguel's eyes sparkled. Disregarding Marina's chiding tone, he reined in, motioning to Lan, who stopped, too. Miguel glanced around. His eye lit on a low-growing clump of sage twenty horse-lengths away. He pointed to it, then to himself, and lastly, with a challenging laugh, to Lan. Nudging his mount into a gallop, Miguel sped towards the bush. Bent completely from the saddle, he caught up a handful of the ash-green foliage. Waving it like a triumphant flag, he cantered back to Lan and Marina. And waited.

Lan, with an effort, controlled his face. Like all Comanche boys he had played at racing past objects and picking them up. This was good training for riding on one side of the horse during warfare with only the heel hooked over its back visible to the enemy. But that bush was only a few inches from the ground and Friend might not care for such antics. A failure before Miguel would be worse than the times Lan had rolled through the dust accompanied by Yellow Wolf's sneering laughter. At least those disasters had not taken place before this strange girl, Marina, who had the valor of a man and watched him confidently. Why should she care, anyway? Was it like her sympathy for the galled bay?

Lan set his heels in Friend's gaunt ribs. As they thundered off, Lan arched down, clinging with legs and thighs and one hand. The ground was a blur, there was the small bush, his fingers stretching. The smell of crushed aromatic leaves stung his nostrils as he straightened. With a negligent show of the bush, he tossed it away as casually as if he had not sweated from the moment Miguel made the challenge.

Miguel shrugged. He rode on, but Marina brought her trim black mare close to Lan.

"*Bueno!*" she smiled. He knew that must mean he had done well. She rode beside him, then, pointing out things and calling their names in Spanish. Lan echoed her. The sooner he knew what was being said around him, the better.

In this level, monotonous country, it did not take long to run out of things to identify. Then Marina began on herself. Lan learned the words for eye, arm, hand, mouth, face, head, foot. Miguel, who had dropped back as if jealous of Marina, cut in with a scornful smile.

Touching his hair, he pointed to his sheathed knife and said something barking, harsh. Marina flushed.

"*Cabello,*" she told Lan swiftly, touching her hair. Miguel snorted. He made a circling motion, then a ripping one on his scalp. He waved this imaginary trophy in Lan's face.

"Yes!" blazed Lan, bursting out in Comanche for he could no longer endure this boy. "I would like to scalp you! And you wouldn't have hair now if I hadn't hindered Yellow Wolf!"

He struck down Miguel's taunting hand. Miguel's eyes contracted. He spun his horse right into Friend, grappling at Lan. Pulling Friend to the side, Lan kicked at Miguel, caught for his neck. They fell to the ground in a scramble of legs and arms, rolling in and out under the nervously stamping horses.

Weak from his fast and exertions since then, Lan felt at once that Miguel was the stronger, heavier. But Lan was the angriest. He had been one of the best wrestlers in his tribe. As a sharp elbow ground into his stomach, Lan gasped for breath, twisted to avoid hands that groped for his throat, caught an arm. Pinning this beneath his enemy, Lan wrenched it till a muffled grunt came from Miguel whose body convulsed to be free of the pain. Lan set his arm around the other's neck in a choking hold.

Air cut off, unable to move without getting a broken arm, Miguel thrashed with his feet, twisted his head, trying somehow to break free.

"Give up," Lan panted, forgetting the other boy could not understand. "Give up or I'll snap your arm!"

The screams he had dimly heard above them turned into a spate of raging commands. The squaw. Well, let her mind her own business! Lan bent the arm he held a little. Miguel groaned.

Something crashed on Lan's head. Bursting red pain shot through him. Dazed, he let go of Miguel, put his hand to his forehead. It came away dripping. He looked through the blood running down his eyebrow to the girl, who, small as she was, seemed to tower above him.

One white-knuckled hand gripped the loaded quirt. Its handle had gashed his skull. Her other hand clutched her leather skirt.

"*Bruto!*" She quivered like a young tree in a high wind. "*Bárbaro!*" Fear and anger darkened her eyes. "Comanche!"

Lan got her meaning. Scrubbing blood from his eye, he gave Miguel a prod with his toe—just to demonstrate what he thought of Mexicans, and dragged himself to the saddle. As he rode off, he heard the squaw's soft, concerned voice, Miguel's brusque one.

They would go, of course, and whine to Blanco, maybe even get him sent back to the blue-coats and that white boys' school. Lan could see how things would go from now on. Miguel would pick fights and when he got them—as he would! —Marina would side with him and they would run to Blanco.

A thick lump rose in Lan's throat. He swallowed angrily. What could you expect from people like that? He touched his throbbing head and could not keep back a grim laugh. Yellow Wolf should see him. He had a scalp that was bloody now, not just red.

Listening for hoofbeats that would tell him that the pair behind him was riding for Blanco, Lan heard them begin. But they moved towards him, not away. He neither hurried nor slowed Friend's pace. If Miguel wanted to take it up again, that was fine. So long as that squaw kept properly out of things.

"*Hola!*"

Did Miguel's shout, though embarrassed, hold warmth? Lan slowly turned. He followed Miguel's pointing arm.

There in the brush was a stirring. A tusked, bristly face showed for an instant. Miguel, rope out, was pelting for the thicket, Marina close behind. Lan slipped his rope from the saddle and rode, too. He crashed into the brush to the right of the others, saw from the corner of one eye that Miguel already had a rope on one squealing, gnashing brush-hog and was choking it down, while Marina caught its feet with her noose. Lan made after a disappearing tail, cast the old rope, and missed. The mesquite grew too thick to follow.

Dodging thorns, he disgustedly wheeled Friend in time to see the brush-hog lunge at Miguel who had got down to cut its throat.

🖋 🖋 🖋 *Amigos*

Lan acted without thought. As the prong-tusked brute thrust at Miguel, knocking him down and laying open the tough leather pants down the length of one thigh, Lan hurled himself off Friend, grabbed the boar from behind by the wire-haired throat and hauled it backwards, locking his knees around its struggling underbody. Tusks made murderous stabs at him. He could not hold the writhing, razor-spined creature long.

"Miguel!" he shouted.

Above the wild thrashing, he could not hear Miguel moving. Was he unconscious? Lan felt his arms weakening, the coarse body turning more violently with each wrench. One of those tusks had to get him in a minute, he was losing his grasp—

A warm fountain gushed over Lan. The hog gave a convulsive leap, yanked Lan sideways, and lay still. Shaken but unhurt, Lan crawled from beneath the beast. Miguel had ripped its throat from one side to the other. He stood panting, blood dripping from his leg. But he grinned at Lan, put out a sticky hand.

"*Gracias.*"

"*Gracias,*" Lan echoed. Whatever Miguel was saying to him, he deserved it back double. Dropping to his knees, Lan pulled apart the torn flaps of the trouser, studying the wound.

It was not deep, but it was long, and tusks were often poi-sonous. Lan pressed hard to make the gash bleed freely. Ma-rina, after one frightened look, was already knocking thorns off a prickly pear leaf and splitting it open. She pressed the pulpy slices against the cut, and motioned for Lan to hold them. Drawing the leather pants leg tight over the cactus poultice, Marina tugged loose her hair ribbon, bound it around and over the pads. When she got up, Lan saw she had bitten her lip cruelly, but she did not cry or act foolish.

Together they got Miguel into his saddle. He looked at the hog and spoke to Marina. Starting his horse back toward camp, she bent to take off the ropes. Lan did it for her. He lifted the hog and tied it by its feet over the back of the blood-excited and fidgeting *maana*. Soon they caught up with Miguel. Lan wished he could ask how the other felt. Strange. They had ridden out enemies.

Now, after a fight and a brush with death in which each saved the other, they came back friends. When one has a friend, one wants to talk with him. Lan really did not think the wound could be serious unless the tusk started a fever, but he wanted to let Miguel know he cared. Maybe that did not take words, though. Going out, they had ridden apart from each other. Now they were as close as possible without bumping.

In camp, they changed the poultice. Marina got a clean white blouse of hers and used it for a bandage. By the time Blanco and the others filtered back to camp with their quarry, Miguel, propped against his saddle, was downing sage tea, making faces and pleas which Javier and Marina ignored.

Blanco, tossing down a white-tailed deer, hurried to examine the wound and ask questions. Redoing the bandage, he nodded evident approval of what they had done.

Suddenly he noticed what Lan had not—the reddish bruises around Miguel's throat. Lan, seeing them now, felt himself turn red. Blanco's query brought a shrug and only a few words from

Miguel who shot Lan a warning glance as the mustanger chief turned to him.

"And how did you get that cut over your eye?" Blanco demanded. "And those scratches on your face?"

Lan gulped. "I—I fell off my horse." In a way, it was true.

Did Blanco's sinewy hand brush across his face to conceal a smile? "Strange. That is how Miguel explains those bruise marks on his neck. I guess we had better watch out for these falls!"

He went over to supervise the disposal of the game. Lan, catching Miguel's discomfitted expression, had to laugh. Blanco had a good idea of what had happened—and a good idea that it would not again. They had not fooled him at all.

For the next three days, the mustangers hunted, dressed their kill, and cut most of the meat into thin strips which they "jerked" in the sun. The result was almost leather tough, but it kept well and was nourishing. Miguel, because of his wound, and Lan, so that he might learn the language, stayed in camp and helped Javier with drying the meat and scraping the hides of the deer after they had been soaked on the hair side with a mixture of water and wood ashes.

"I will make moccasins and bags out of the little skins," said Javier. "But these three big hides will make clothing, and must be carefully tanned and worked. Save all the brains and liver for the tanning."

Remembering the weeks his mother sometimes spent on a hide, Lan made a face. "I can see this camp is going to stink for a long time!"

"You'll be chasing horses most of the time," Javier retorted. "When you wear out those pants on the cactus, don't come to me for a new pair."

"You can make them?"

"I learned many things among the Comanches."

Lan snapped his fingers. All the time during the hunt he had longed for a bow, and while cleaning one of the bucks, he had thought what a good bowstring the tendons that ran along its spine would make. Hopefully, he had saved the sinew, sure he would find some use for it though he lacked the expert skill required to shape a bowstring. He knelt earnestly by Javier, lighting the cigarette the old man had just rolled and presenting it to him respectfully.

"Javier, wise one, could you make me a bow? After the fashion of The People?"

"Plainly. If I wished to." The old face wrinkled even more. "But why do either of us think of Comanches? I will make you a good rope. That is the hunting mode of the mustangers."

Significantly glancing at Miguel, Lan said, "It has its drawbacks. With a bow, I could kill at a distance. Maybe bring you some quail or doves."

"And show off to Miguel and Marina?" Javier laughed. He thought a minute. "Look, I will make the bow string if you save some good tendons. I have some arrowheads I saved as curiosities and I will fix these on shafts. Someone will surely bag a turkey. We will use his feathers to wing the arrows. That is all I'll have time to do. You make the bow."

"Well—I can try. Maybe your string will make up for my mistakes." Rising, Lan unconsciously looked around for a bois d'arc or hickory tree. When he saw nothing but mesquite and ebony, he remembered what he should have thought of at once. There was no timber close which would make bow wood. Only the hardest, most perfectly straight-grained wood could serve.

"Think of something?" asked Javier.

With a gloomy nod, Lan pointed at the gnarled mesquites. "They won't make arrows, much less bows."

"No. But ash will make both."

"While we're dreaming, so would mulberry," said Lan.

"Ah, but we don't have mulberry. And if we were only

dreaming, would we not make dogwood arrows and bois d'arc bow, the very best?" Javier blew out a curl of strong smoke, enjoying Lan's puzzlement. "I do have ash, seasoned at that, in the cart. I always bring enough to carve several yokes which I sell when we return to the settlements."

Lan caught a quick breath of relief. "I must pay you, wise one. But how?"

"Don't worry about that." Javier's few teeth showed in mirth. "By the time you get those hides shaved of hair and scraped smooth of every bit of flesh, you'll think you've earned enough bows to outfit the whole band of Honey-Eaters!"

Well, it was worth squaw work to get a bow. Lan brought the tendons to Javier. Then he joined Miguel at "fleshing" the hides which were pegged to the ground. With their knives, they shaved away every particle of fat, meat, and blood, spreading wet ashes on the fatty surface once in a while.

"I hope," growled Miguel, looking up through his tangle of black hair and the sweat that dripped from his eyebrows, "that we go after horses tomorrow!" Lan didn't understand all the words, but he read the eloquent gestures which accompanied them, and grinned.

Miguel had suffered no infection from the boar's tusk and moved stiffly only after getting up in the morning or sitting still a long time. Blanco's orders kept him at Javier's disposal, but The Monkey wanted to be off tearing through the brush, snaring things with his wonderful rope.

When the hunters came in that evening, Blanco dumped his buck on the ground and held up his hand for quiet. Javier translated in Lan's ear.

"We have meat enough for a week," he announced. "This afternoon, Chon and his group saw mustangs. They must be the ones that usually water here returning to see if their land is now safe. In the morning we will go after them."

Lan yelled applause with the others. The sooner this bunch

was secured, the sooner would begin the chase after the Ghost, which, if successful, would mean Lan's freedom—return to The People, vengeance on Yellow Wolf!

Tired though they were, the hunters cleaned their kill that night to cut down on what Javier would have to do unaided. Lan collected all the deer brains and liver in an earthenware jug, covering it with a weighted-down piece of hide to keep out scavengers like the coyotes who were howling along with Chon's guitar. The more work he saved Javier, the sooner he'd have his arrows and bowstring.

That night, while Chon sang his *Ay-ay-ay-ay*, Javier brought out to Lan a length of ash about three feet long. "I cut off part of it for arrows, but this should be about bow size. It's too dark to work on that hide. Try this for a while."

Lan very happily left the pegged hide, its faint smell of decayed flesh. Eyes screwed in concentration, he shaved and sliced and smoothed at the wood. Marina stood watching some minutes, then, pointing at the stick, said a word Lan knew.

"What?"

He pantomimed for her the curving pull, the zing of the arrow. She clapped and laughed, sitting down to watch. Presently, Miguel, too, joined them, questioned, and settled to respectful attention.

Lan felt pleased at their interest, and also nervous. This bow had better be good. He had made play bows, of course, even some rather accurate ones. But on this one hinged the honor of The People. He wished again he had some medicine.

One lucky thing, it did not take medicine to chase mustangs, as they would tomorrow. Only that Ghost—it might take medicine for him. Yes, it surely would.

Before they left camp next morning, the mustangers carefully removed all suspicious signs from near the corral and the eastern approach to it. The cart and the pegged hides were out of sight and range of the horses' imagined course. The mules, bell mares, and extra horses were hobbled to prevent their joining their wild kin.

"You stay with Marina and Miguel," Blanco told Lan as they saddled. "Chon is our *encerrador*. Felipe, the Sauz brother who is both lean and short, is his helper, the *cortador*. They will bar the gate after the mustangs are in, and if there should be too many horses for the pen, they must scare away the extras so they don't pour in and trample the rest."

Lan nodded, impatient to be off. He saddled Friend and was waiting when Inglés rode by. The big yellow-haired man rode a horse the shade of his hair except that perhaps the horse was cleaner. Lan stared at the long scars on the golden horse's shoulder.

Claw marks? As Miguel joined him, Lan jerked his head towards the horse and touched his own shoulder as if to scratch it. "What?" he asked in Spanish. As Miguel's gaze followed Lan's, it narrowed. He made his hand like a claw.

"Inglés—*onza*, lion. Marks horses."

Lan twisted in his saddle. "Inglés?" He made a slashing motion at Friend's shoulder.

Miguel shrugged. His arm circled the mustangers. "We believe it. Blanco, no."

Did Miguel mean that Inglés was a bad medicine man who could turn into a lion and maltreat his animals? Had anyone seen him do this? Lan buzzed with questions, but his Spanish was too poor for such involved matters. He would ask Javier. Lan's scalp prickled to see how Inglés sat his saddle with lazy grace, like, indeed, a giant cat.

My one real enemy here, Lan thought. *And he has to be a sorcerer!*

Blanco in the lead, the band moved up the valley. They would veer a long way northeast so as to come up behind the mustangs and be in position to drive them towards the pen. Keeping together, they rode till the sun came down at a late morning slant, hot and piercing in their eyes. Blanco dropped back.

"You sharp-eyed young ones can ride scout and watch for the herd," he told Lan in Comanche. "Stay separated but close enough to signal." The leader repeated this to his daughter and godson who gave a united, joyous whoop, and soared to the sides and ahead of the main group of mustangers.

Lan, urging Friend with his knees, soon took the right-hand point. Marina had the middle and Miguel the left. How good it was to be out in front, free of dust, and able to see for unbroken miles over the grassy flats. Lan could almost imagine that he was an advance for a war party . . .

"Hola!"

In the same instant of Miguel's shout, Lan saw the dust. Far to the left, it looked like a low white cloud. Soft shouts came from the mustangers. Lan became a far edge of a wide-flung net, Miguel and Marina once more beside him. Evidently Blanco did not want to crowd the wild runners yet, but slowly close in on them as they approached the corral.

It was like watching a dream turn to reality, getting near enough to see the horses in the wafting dust. Roan, sorrel, gray, dun, blood bay, spotted, they floated in the sunlit haze like cloud creatures, beautiful in their mane-tossing freedom. Many colts were in the herd, foaled that spring, legging alongside their mothers, whickering plaintively, their fuzzy tails bouncing.

From the size of this herd, Lan would have known the stallion was unusual even if a driving black devil had not suddenly whipped from the far side to prod the laggards. Only the fittest stallions had mares at all, and few of them controlled a harem of over fifteen to twenty.

This black, with his masterful handling, showed why he was

worthy to lead such a *manada*. Nipping the slow ones, coursing at the sides, he kept them together, a feat which would have required dozens of men, for unshepherded mustangs scattered like quail when alarmed.

The herd was tiring, though, worn down by exile from their accustomed range and water. The colts particularly could not keep up. The stallion had to bite, knock forcefully against the mares, rip hide from their rumps and shoulders to keep them going.

Lan was glad it was not far to the corral now. In another half-hour, if all went well, the proud black and his band would be inside brush walls. They were entering the mouth of the valley.

A colt dropped back. Its mother turned, nuzzling it, coaxing. Its legs buckled. It fell. Back swept the stallion.

Ramming the mare in the ribs, he shoved her after the herd. She whinnied and tried to circle back. He grabbed her haunch with his teeth, kicked her. Harrying, forcing her to move, he stayed close till she was absorbed in the group before he swung out to chasten other weary ones.

The colt lay as if his legs were broken. As the mustangers neared, he tried to climb up, fell back on his knobby knees, and watched them. Lan stopped before it. Marina was down perhaps a second earlier, and Miguel made a third wall to the protective fence they made about the little black fellow.

A motion, a glint of metal, caught Lan's eye. Inglés was sighting down his rifle, aiming between Miguel and Lan. Lan, with a touch of his heels, sent Friend crashing against Inglés' horse. The rifle went off in the air.

Before Inglés could more than snarl one raging word, Blanco rode between, catching the blond man's bridle. He spoke with soft emphasis. Slowly, smoldering, Inglés scabbarded his rifle. His light eyes drilled into Lan a moment before he looped his golden horse and rode after the other mustangers.

That left the three young people looking helplessly down at the colt. He was so exhausted that if they left him here the coyotes and vultures would feast. Still, he weighed a hundred pounds; he would not fit over somebody's saddle.

Marina brought her hands together. She took her rope from the saddle, bubbling with a plan of which Lan could only catch a few words. As she started doubling the rope, and making signs, he began to understand. In a few minutes, his rope and Miguel's had joined Marina's to form a sort of broad webbed band with long ends. Marina padded the middle of this with her sash. Then, while Lan and Miguel got the colt to his feet, she tied one end of the contrivance to her saddle horn, passed the broad, padded part under the colt's belly. Miguel mounted. Lan handed him the other end of the combined ropes. Marina got on her mare and they started off at a careful pace, Lan at the rear.

The colt, thus supported, had to move. He whickered piteously to say he did not like it. Why had his mother left him to such indignities?

"Little brother," Lan called, laughing softly, "little brother, it will be all right. Your soft eyes will not feed the crows tonight anyhow."

In twenty minutes they were in sight of the herd which was just opposite the corral. Twisting in the saddle, Miguel pointed ahead.

"We—" he motioned to himself and Lan, "go!"

They loosed the ropes from Miguel's saddle. Leaving Marina to keep the colt, the two boys pelted down the valley. They reached the fringe of mustangers in time to see the black stallion stop trying to move his herd.

He turned, waited, facing the line of men.

⩣ ⩣ ⩣ Little Devil

Ears laid back, great mouth open, the stallion defied his pursuers. Blanco rode forward. Forcing him back, the black charged. He had plainly determined to retreat no further.

Without his leadership, it would be almost impossible to pen the mares. Blanco whipped out his carbine, loaded, and called an order. He, Inglés, and the two other men possessed of guns, fired into the air above the horses.

The stallion curvetted, but stood his ground. They faced each other, the wild horses and men almost as wild. Softly, Blanco called, "Miguel. Lázaro!" Miguel borrowed a rope.

They rode to the front, shaping their ropes as did Blanco. While the mustanger chief rode straight at the black, Miguel cast for the stallion's forefeet in an underhanded toss, and Lázaro, the skinny Sauz brother, sent his *reata* over its neck.

Miguel's rope missed, but as the black came at Blanco, teeth bared, Lázaro's toss held and Blanco neatly socked the hind feet in either loop of an 8-shaped figure. The stallion fell hard, flailing with its front feet, trying to rise. Miguel caught the forefeet with a new throw and the king stallion was snared. Blanco turned his rope over to Lan and led the other mustangers after the wildly-fleeing herd.

It would have been hopeless to drive the mares far without

their master, but this close to the corral, there was a chance. Lan watched as the men hurtled alongside the mares, whirling ropes, shouting. The lead mares were almost even with the brush wings. If they would just turn down those lanes . . .

But the lead mare shied. She dodged between a horseman and the brush wall, veering to the side. That did it. The following horses tore after her. The men had to move or be stampeded. Panicked beyond control, the mustangs surged past the wings, past the corral, speeding down the river bed and along the valley slopes till capture would have been a matter of running down each individual horse and roping it. One by one, the men gave up the useless chase. Blanco rode back to the three he had left with the stallion. Taking his own rope back from Lan, he signaled Miguel and Lázaro. Lázaro loosed the black's head, Miguel shook off the loosened front rope, and when the stallion lunged up, Blanco retrieved the cast-off loop from the back feet. With a mighty shake, the horse galloped off after his scattered *manada*.

"Why did you let him go?" Lan puzzled. "He's a fine horse, valiant."

Blanco gazed after the swiftly vanishing black. "We'll give him time to gather his herd. Then we'll try again to catch the whole bunch. If we kept him, we'd never have the mares unless they turned up in other *manadas* we captured."

More delay. Why, the Ghost could die of old age before they took his trail! Some of Lan's vexation sounded in his question.

"If stallions are so important to manage a drove, why don't you use tame ones to take the place of wild leaders?"

"I've tried that. A tame horse usually can't control wild ones and if he's left long with them, some real herd stallion will run off all the mares." Blanco shook his head admiringly. "That black is one fine animal. I want him for myself."

You'll have to catch him first. Lan remembered Marina and the little colt that had probably been sired by the black. Turning, Lan saw her far down the valley. He explained to Blanco, who grinned.

"Help her bring him to camp. At least we caught one horse today!"

When Lan and Miguel got back to Marina and the abandoned colt, she had taken the rope support from beneath him and he was teetering about on his long, bony legs. Marina had seen what happened at the corral and did not ask any questions, but returned their coiled ropes to the boys, and got on her mare.

They started to camp. The colt trotted in front of them, circling as if hunting his mother and familiar manes and tails. When he did not find them, he took off in a straight line, jolting indignantly, his short mane and tail flopping like hair on a waved coup stick. He whinnied and listened and pawed with his dainty black hooves for all the world like a child whose mother had not come immediately when it cried. Lan chuckled, but he felt sorry for the wispy small creature.

"*Diablito!*" Marina said, smiling at the colt. Miguel nodded. So did Lan, though he would have to wait till they got to camp to learn what the name meant.

At the camp, Diablito strayed around, investigating the other horses. At last, convinced he was a stranger, he stood still and nickered forlornly. Marina had mixed brown sugar, ground corn, and water into a gruel. She came toward the colt, holding out the shallow bowl. He threw down his head, upped his heels, and fled.

Lan caught him, sinking down in a scramble of legs and hoofs. "Hua, little one," he murmured. "Hua, small brother."

It stopped struggling though it quivered against him. He spoke to it again in his secret voice and it watched him, velvety eyes swimming. Then it nuzzled at him hungrily. Lan said, "No, you must make friends with Marina. She has your food."

He beckoned to her with a bend of his head and she came up quietly in her moccasins. Lan talked to the colt while she dipped her finger in the gruel and let it taste, gradually coaxed it to drink from the bowl. Relief flashed like sunlight in Marina's smile. From the corner of his eye, Lan saw Javier limping over.

"*Ay,* the small orphan," cackled the *reatero.* He squatted to look over the colt. "Not much to show for a whole herd, is he? If that mare had gone down the wing— But that's mustanging. How did you get this one?"

"He couldn't keep up with the herd. His name is Diablito. What does that mean?"

"Little Devil." Though no one could understand them except Blanco, Javier dropped his voice. "Keep him clear of Inglés. The blond likes a tender colt steak and besides he's grinding his teeth over the loss of that herd."

Lan had eaten horse meat. He did not recoil at that, but at the notion of Inglés getting this one particular little colt now snuggled in his arms. "Diablito's ours! Inglés knows it."

"All the more reason he'd do it. He doesn't like anybody, but he hates Indians."

Know how your enemy thinks, Arrow In His Shield had used to counsel. *It will aid you more than a strong shield.* Stroking the colt, Lan asked, "Why does he hate us?"

"They say Inglés was one of Lafitte's men—Lafitte was a robber who stole from ships on the great water. Anyhow, once when these robbers were at Padre Island, a gang of Karankawa Indians got hold of Inglés' brother. They ate him—or that's the story."

"Karankawas!" Lan spat out the dirty name. "They live like mud turtles. And they do eat men. Comanches despise cannibals. That's why we fight the Tonkawas."

"No importance to Inglés."

Glancing at the big catlike man, Lan felt a chill go up his

spine. He remembered the marks on the golden horse. "Javier, how did Inglés' horse get those clawprints on its shoulder?"

Wrinkles formed thickly around the old eyes. "Why do you ask that?"

"Miguel—I did not understand. But he seemed to mean that Inglés made the scars himself, that—he changed into a lion or—is the word *onza*."

"*Onza?*" Javier started violently. "Don't even think of it! Inglés did make those marks. He calls it his sign and does it by fitting steel tips to his fingers, or so I have heard. A foolish conceit, that is all."

Lan persisted, "What is an *onza?*"

It seemed for a moment that Javier was going to stalk off. He shut his mouth on words twice, then sighed. "It is bad luck to talk of *onzas*. One might hear and plague us. But so that you will cease such questions, I'll explain. An *onza* is a great cat that is not really a cat."

"What is it, then?" asked Lan impatiently.

"Shh! It is a witch, a bad shaman that can take cat form. *Muy malo.* Very bad."

The prickles crawled up Lan's spine again. "How do you know Inglés isn't one? That coffee of his might be his medicine."

"Most gringos drink coffee and they never heard of *onzas*. No, Inglés would like people to think that of him and be more afraid than they are. The main reason I'm sure he is not one is that he acts as if he were."

Lan grunted. "That is mixed up, wise one. It does not sound reasonable."

"Task me with that when people become reasonable." Javier stood up. "Diablito is full. Now you must eat."

That night while the mustangers rested and planned for the morrow, Lan worked on his bow, shaping the ash to the proper size. Diablito stayed near him, a little way off in the shadow.

Miguel sat watching Lan and Javier, but Marina crooned to the colt the way some mothers sang to their babies. For the first time since he had come to know her, Lan felt she did not belong in this camp. She really was a woman and should be with them. But if she had no mother— Lan turned from that puzzle to another.

"Javier, how did Inglés come to join Blanco?"

The old man had evaded this question before, but he might feel now that Lan deserved an answer. Javier cleared his throat, evidently thinking back. "I told you Inglés was with Lafitte, the sea robber. Well, finally the gringo government ran him out of Galvez town. That's where the white boys' school is now. The gang split up. Inglés lived a while in Matamoros, then traveled to New Mexico and threw in with some Comancheros."

"The Mexican traders who deal with Comanches?"

"Yes. As you may know, they sometimes ransom white captives and return them to their people. Twelve years ago, they traded with a band that had as prisoners Blanco's wife and their baby, Marina. Inglés bought them from the Indians. The woman was sick. She told him who her husband was and where their home rancho was in case Inglés failed to locate Blanco in the brushlands. She died on the way, but Inglés brought the baby girl safely to her father."

"Blanco hadn't known his family was stolen?"

Javier's mouth made a grim, tight line. "He had left them well while he and his group went to mustang. A lot can happen in three months on the frontier. And Comanches strike like lightning and go like the wind. No, Blanco had thought all was good with his pretty young wife and their three-year-old daughter. Can you blame him for trying to see the best in Inglés, even though it means shutting both eyes?"

"Why didn't Inglés go back to the Comancheros?"

"He had quarreled with them about something. Besides,

Blanco offered him a high share of his profits and half the income of his home ranch. Besides, if Inglés stayed much in the towns his temper and reputation would get him killed. He knows that."

Lan said nothing. Inglés did not seem the kind of man to go to any trouble returning stolen children, but that was a matter of which Blanco was the best judge. How strange that Blanco did not hate Comanches, after all his suffering from them! Lan realized with a shock that he was beginning to like the white-haired man who had enslaved him.

After a while, Lan spread his blanket beyond the cart. He was scarcely settled when he felt an awkward body sprawl next to him. The salty, pleasant smell of horse came to him and he smiled. Marina might feed the colt, but Lan had talked to him and breathed in his nostrils. That was one thing neither Yellow Wolf nor the blue-coat colonel nor the mustangers could take away even though he was a red-haired Comanche with no medicine. He had the horse-talk.

Beside him the colt heaved a sighing snort. "Small one," Lan whispered, "a lot has happened to you today. But you'll be all right." He touched the short frizzy mane and closed his eyes, feeling a good tiredness. The colt might be Diablito to the camp but to Lan he was Little Brother.

Next morning, in the first faint light, everybody got up. Marina fed Diablito with Lan's help. After a breakfast of sweetened corn mush and seared meat, Blanco rubbed his hands on his knees and came to his feet in one motion.

"We'll see if the stallion has his herd collected. It won't do to let them get rested. We'll split into groups and scout the country. You come with me, Lan." He spoke to Marina and Miguel in Spanish which Lan understood enough to know they were being told to accompany Blanco, too.

As Lan started off, Diablito squealed and rushed jerkily

after him. Javier swiftly fashioned a rope halter, tossed it to Lan. "Bring that wild *caballo* back here and I'll tend him," the *reatero* said.

Lan hitched the little fellow to the cart axle. "Be good, now. Maybe we will find your mother." One could make any promise to an animal because it did not understand and could not be disappointed. All Diablito sensed was the warmth in Lan's voice, and for Lan it was enough communication to know how eagerly the colt watched him, even while Marina patted him good-by.

Splitting into three groups which took different directions, the mustangers rode steadily all that day without stopping to rest or eat, chewing their jerky while in the saddle.

"I don't like to use our horses this way," Blanco said. "But if we don't locate that herd, they'll soon leave this range."

"What if they do get away?" Lan wondered.

"Hunt another bunch." Blanco swallowed the jerky he had been chewing the past fifteen minutes and drank from his canteen, offering it to Lan who drank thankfully. Jerky was strong food but tasted like an old moccasin. "The colonel wants all the horses I can get him. He has the responsibility of supplying several other forts with remounts."

"What does the colonel give you for these horses? Guns?"

"No, money. It is easy to carry and I can get what I want with it."

Puzzled, Lan asked, "Have you some with you? What does it look like?" Perhaps it was a rare food or costly herb.

Blanco drew from his shirt a small pouch. He shook out a large silver disc and a smaller gold one. "See? In this little pouch I can carry the value of many herds, many guns. I do not have the bother of cumbersome things till I actually need them, and with money I can buy at the most convenient place."

"Some of our braves use the silver money for ornaments," Lan said, unable to hide his disappointment. "I would rather have horses or robes or food. Unless someone would trade these for your money, you could have a *tipi* of it and still starve or freeze!"

"True." Blanco slanted an amused look at Lan. "Money has value only because people have decided it does. But as long as they will give me supplies for it, I will not argue."

Lan shrugged. "The money is pretty but I do not trust it. It is better to trade as Comanches do."

"That is also done. But sometimes a man has something to sell when he does not want to buy, or he needs to buy when he has nothing to trade. Money is a way of storing supplies handily till they are needed."

"It is delusion. I do not think it can last long."

"Lad," Blanco chuckled, "money has been used for many more years than white people have been in this country. Our Lord was sold for thirty pieces of silver. And the priest says that was long generations before the *conquistadores* saw Mexico."

"Who is Our Lord?"

Blanco's eyebrows shot up. He looked almost afraid. Then, studying Lan, he spoke carefully. "He was the Son of the Great Spirit. He lived on earth as a man. Bad men killed Him but He went back to His Father in heaven."

"He is still there?"

"Of a certainty!"

Lan pondered. "The People do not have any story about the Great Spirit's Son. Are you sure Our Lord was not just a strong medicine man?"

Blanco's hand moved rapidly down his face and across his breast. "You were raised a heathen and cannot be blamed, but do not say such things! Our Lord *was* a great medicine man. He raised the dead and cured the blind. But He was also the Son of the Great Spirit. I should have sent you to the mission school. It is bitter that you, white and probably baptized, have no knowledge of the true faith. And I am too ignorant to instruct you properly."

"Baptized—what is that?"

Eyes narrowing, Blanco muttered some scandalized words. Then, with a real effort to speak calmly, he said, "When you were born, your parents doubtless took you before a priest—a kind of medicine man—and he blessed you in the Great Spirit's name and sprinkled you with water."

"That's it!" Lan cried, suddenly understanding.

"What?" Blanco's voice took on a tinge of hope. "You surely don't remember—"

"No, but the medicine spirits would! That's why none of them came to me. They knew white man's power had already been called for me. But—" It tore bitterly from Lan's throat and his eyes stung. "This white man's medicine is no good to me! I am a Comanche."

"Be silent!" Blanco leaned forward, his lips a pale line. "Speak like that again and I will send you to the priests at Galveston as should have been done at the start! May I be forgiven that I did not think of your heathen raising when I offered to keep you!"

Lan bit his lip. He was genuinely scared. Blanco seemed horrified enough to pack him off at a breath to that eastern school. It was that the mustanger felt he had done wrong in not attending to Lan's religious training in the white man's faith. Lan swallowed.

The Great Spirit might have had a Son, in which case it would be well to know about Him. "I will hear what you say," Lan promised. "Only do not break your word. You said you would keep me if I would not run away."

"That is so." Blanco rubbed his forehead. He brightened. "Life with us will make it easier for you to learn when you finally are near folk who can teach you."

Lan kept quiet. The mustangers' camp was as close to the white man's civilization as he wanted to get, ever.

The sun crawled down the western sky. They had found tracks and droppings several times that day but if the stallion had made them, he had circled and retraced and cut his own trail so many times they were hopeless for tracking.

As Lan figured it, they had circled in a wide half-loop and were southeast of the corral by some miles. It would be dark in two hours. Gazing west, Lan saw the horizon moving. Had the far rim of earth come alive?

Once before he had seen something like that. Yes, the time he had seen that huge herd of buffalo, a vast brown blanket far as the eye could reach. But this was too far southeast for them. He rode next to Blanco, pointing.

"Mustangs?"

⚑ ⚑ ⚑ *Stampede*

Blanco stared. He shaded his eyes and his strong hand trembled. "Yes—hundreds! And look! Aren't those riders coming up from the side?" Shielding his gaze, Lan watched the small figures till he was sure.

"Yes, two of them."

"Perhaps Chon and Lázaro," hoped Blanco. "We'll need them at the corral to turn off all but about two hundred. If these keep running the way they are, they'll head right into the wings. Our worry will be to prevent a pile-up."

Cupping his hands, he gave a long piercing whistle. It came back faintly from the distant riders.

"Our men," said Blanco in relief. "The others must be at the flank of the mustangs. We might as well wait till they come abreast. All we can do with this stampede is try to stem it when it's filled our pen."

"So many!" Lan breathed, watching the tossing mass form into discernible horses. Marina, too, sat spellbound, and Miguel fingered his rope.

"Myself, I have seen such numbers only a few times," Blanco said. "It happens when a number of *manadas* are panicked and run together till they calm. Prairie fire may cause it, or even just the scent of a lion."

"How do they sort themselves out?"

"Leave that to the stallions! When the fright's over, they cut their herd, each and all, out of the rest, and trot off to their own range."

Chon and Lázaro shot past, waving. As *encerrador* and *cortador*, they had to outrun the stampede, be hidden behind the brush wings when the mustangs ran down them. Chon pointed backwards, shouted.

"*—otros,*" was all they caught. Lan knew the word, others. The main group of the mustangers must be trailing the mustangs.

The outrunners of these swept by now. All colors, their legs obscured in fine dust, they were like creatures from a medicine dream. Running, running, it seemed they would trample the prairies till the whole earth was a revolving whirl of manes and tails and driving power. Lan, deafened, felt the pound of hoofs with his own heartbeat. Blood pumped through him to the surging rhythm as Friend took up the chase beside Blanco. Marina and Miguel bent low to their horses' manes on the right, and coming fast through the sifting dust were the other mustangers. Later they could tell how they chanced to sight this herd and, if they knew, tell what had started the vast running together of *manadas*, usually so jealously guarded by their master stallions. But for now, it was just to speed on the wind, breathing dust, horse, maybe even sunlight, and the whole world running with you.

Over the flats, past scatters of trees, sighting the river bed from the slope, then the plunge into the valley. Narrowing, narrowing, oh, why could the run not last forever? Up ahead where the dust-hazed bulks of corral and wings, the shape of Javier's cart beyond. Lan saw them because he knew they were there; he had seen them obscured like this before. But the mustangs, blind with their own dust, would not see anything. Till it was too late.

How they poured now into the wide-mouthed wings, crowd-

87

ing fast! Lacking a single determined leader like the black stallion, the faster mustangs tore thick as they could thrust into the gradually narrowing passage.

Soon, surely, Chon and Lázaro would wave their blankets and shut off the living stream, diverting it past the full corral. Soon— There must be two, maybe three hundred penned. *Chon! Lázaro! Stop them!* Beside him, Lan heard Blanco's shout, saw dread pull taut the captain's face.

Through smarting eyes, blinking back the dust, Lan saw why. The edge of a blanket flailed vainly, desperately. Javier hobbling along the corral with a cloth which he, too, waved. Mustangers galloping along the sides of the herd, trying some-how to cut in and turn them.

There was Marina waving her sash, Miguel slashing with his *reata*. And Blanco ramming home a cartridge, easing back the hammer, fixing the percussion cap in place, and firing over the wild mass. Lan sent Friend towards the wings, but was choked back by the threshing sea of mustangs. He could see Javier, Chon, and Lázaro whipping their blankets, but all they managed was to keep from being trampled themselves. They frightened the near horses but those behind pushed irresist-ibly on.

In the tight press at the mouth of the corral, some went down under the pressure, were leaped upon by those behind who flooded on across the standing horses, kicking, plunging, shifting through the tight-packed confusion. The weaker went down, shrilling, struggling, as the oncoming masses lunged up and across them.

Impelled forward, unable to stop, the first horses into the corral broke into the saplings of the corral walls, splitting them apart, bursting them down. Brush and limbs scattered, splintered, as the living wind surged on.

In minutes the corral was emptied of all but dead and crippled horses. The bulk of the herd coursed down the river bed, the low slopes. There was no use to try to turn them now, even had that been possible. The corral was in ruins except for the brush-heaped wings which had led so many mustangs to death.

Lan could not believe the broken, twisted shapes. He gripped his saddle horn and rocked back and forth because he had to do something or weep. Tears were streaking Blanco's face.

He whistled in his men. Without a word, he and the other men with guns went about the corral, shooting the maimed horses. Many of these were colts.

This was an expensive mercy for ammunition was scarce, but Lan could not watch. Minutes ago was that wild beauty, that dream of boundless speed and grace; now the mangled forms trying to rise, some of them— Lan fought down a rise of scalding vomit. He took his knife and helped dispatch the cripples. It was all he could do for them. He saw Marina bowed in the dust by a fine spotted pony with two broken legs. She held his head and cried as if her heart were breaking while Blanco explained that it must die.

By the time this harsh kindness was finished, it was almost dark. The mustangers straggled to their camp, but few had the will to make fires and eat. Even the few who might possibly not have mourned the useless slaughter were aghast at losing such a fine catch. Inglés had his coffee, everyone smoked, and one by one cut off meat from the latest-killed deer. Javier made his people—Blanco, Miguel, Marina, and Lan—eat thick stew. After forcing the first few swallows, Lan found he was ravenous and ate a second bowl full. He had forgotten Diablito till an impatient whicker came from the shadows behind the cart.

"*Pobrecito!*" Marina was up in an instant. To her, most creatures were "poor little ones," Lan was sure. She mixed *pinole* and water in her bowl, carried it around the cart. Lan followed.

As the colt thrust hungrily at the bowl, almost knocking Marina off balance, Lan had to smile.

He tried in Spanish to tell Marina what he felt. "This—he's not dead. Strong." Lan made a running motion with his fingers. "Will go fast."

Marina looked up. Tears glistened in her eyes, but she smiled as she stroked the jerking mane. "Lan, you talk beautiful Spanish!"

He had never thought to feel good at hearing that. Shock, gratitude, the upheaval of the day closed in on him. He dropped hastily beside Diablito to hide a disgraceful dampness in his eyes.

"Hua," he said, "Hua, baby devil." Jerking its tail, the colt made lusty smacking sounds till all the gruel was gone.

"Come, you two," Blanco called. "We must move out early in the morning." Lan did not have to ask why.

By tomorrow night, the ruined corral would stink for miles. The cultures would feast, and the coyotes, and all the scavengers of the brush. As Lan rolled in his blanket, he seemed to hear the beating hoofs, the dying screams, and all that night he dreamed. Caught in with the mustangs, he tried to climb on living bodies over the wall and fell back as the giant face of Yellow Wolf rose over the horizon, laughing.

"Bloody Scalp, worthless—white-blooded Comanche!"

Lan came slowly awake at the voice, discovered it was not saying what he had heard in his dream.

"Get up!" Javier scolded. "What are you groaning for? You ought to have my rheums and pains and you'd have something to complain about! Now hurry. I must pack my skins, reeking of liver and brains though they are, and you can catch up the mules for me."

Lan speared a piece of meat from the fire, chewed it with a handful of *pinole*. "Where will we go, Javier?"

"There are pens all over this country, more or less broken

down as this one was. We caught a good herd last year in a pen two days' ride west of here. The Corral of the Snakes. We may go there."

"And kill more mustangs?" Lan sprang to his feet, saying what had been pent up in him all night. "It's a foul, dirty business! It's like killing the wind, like—"

Javier's eyes burned suddenly. "Catch up the mules," he whispered as Lan fell silent. Turning, the old man dragged his hamstrung leg as he began to pack the cart. When Lan got back with the team, he saw a pile of manes and tails on top of the half-tanned hides. He looked away, but knew that Javier was only using common sense. The hair would make many fine ropes. And that was not all. At noon, the meat they roasted above crackling mesquite wood was from the mustangs. On the plains man could sorrow, but he could not waste. Lan ate with the others.

Towards evening, they watered at a shallow hole of water seeping up in an arroyo. Large mesquites made grateful shade on the banks. These trees were usually within five miles of water, for their seed was spread mostly by the manure of wild horses who ate the beans and ranged near the hole. At a soft slope of the bank, an old adobe corral seemed to melt into the white dust. In a few seasons it would be gone entirely back to its native clay.

"Why isn't this place used for a pen?" Lan asked Blanco who had ridden most of the day without a word.

Blanco seemed glad of the question. His thoughts could not be happy ones. "No one stops here after dark. This is the Corral of the Dead Ones. Eight mustangers were killed here by Comanches years ago and their spirits haunt the place. They have been heard in the night, wailing and screaming as if in their final torment."

Lan's scalp prickled. The shade of the mesquites, so pleasant a moment earlier now seemed threatening. He was glad when they tightened their saddles and rode on.

He had never personally seen a ghost, but he knew lots of people who had. Everyone knew ghosts hung thick over scenes of battle and disaster. Sometimes medicine men got power from ghosts, but it was dangerous. One young warrior had been chased all night by a skeleton and it was said that much of Thunder Waters' power was derived from secrets told him by a ghost he had wrestled and defeated.

This spectre—a scalped, bloody thing—had jumped on Thunder Waters one night as he made camp. The moon was just rising and that was the time ghosts liked best. Thunder Waters grabbed it and held it down with his knees till it begged and gave him medicine for battle. Lan, badly as he wanted power, thought he would rather do without. If bare bone arms gripped him some night he was sure he would swiftly become a ghost, too. He would die of sheer fright!

Diablito stayed close to Friend's heels. Could his mother have been one of the horses that lay dead in the corral? The great black stallion had not been seen, but some of his strayed band might have been in the mixed *manadas*. Sometimes the small colt cantered to the side and ran in tiny thunder, but he always came back. Lan, watching him, felt deep shame at Diablito's trust of those who had devastated the mustangs.

This must have shown on Lan's face, for Blanco touched his knee. "Listen, boy. Most mustangers figure on losing a third of their catch from the time they're penned till they're tamed. We save four out of five. I do not like their deaths."

"I know you do not." But Lan knew he could never forget the sight of horses struggling to rise on broken legs, lunging in agony.

That night in camp, Miguel and Marina helped Lan with his Spanish while he worked on his bow, rubbing it with fat to make it pliable. Lan was really learning most of the common words and flushed with pleasure at his young teachers' praise. "*Bueno!*" Marina cried. "*Usted habla muy bien!*"

She glanced up as a long shadow gloomed across them. Inglés' smoldering eyes fixed on Lan with hatred Lan felt like a physical blow. "Comanche *malo!*" he blazed. He made a cutting motion across his throat, raised his arm to his mouth and pretended to chew, then pointed to Lan. "Comanche *come hombres.*" Lan got that. *Comanche eat men.* He felt white-hot inside, so furious he was calm.

"No." Lan shook his head. He pointed to Inglés, then to his mouth. "Comanche *no como* Inglés." Pretending to retch, he groped for the Spanish words. "Inglés—dirty. Make sick!"

Inglés snarled. Speechless with anger, he reached for Lan. Marina sprang up. Lan was on his feet, too, the bow ready to use as a club, and Miguel held the rope he could use like magic. Marina raged at the blond. It seemed he might grab her. But Blanco, over by Javier, had turned and was crossing to them.

Cursing, Inglés flung away. Running to her father, Marina poured out the story too fast for Lan fully to understand. Blanco sighed heavily, patting his daughter's head.

"Inglés will hate you in his soul now."

"Comanches don't eat people," Lan cried. "I would like to tear out his forked tongue and choke him with it!"

"Be peaceful," Blanco said. "Dead men do not care about their bodies. Let us sleep so that we may reach the corral early."

They entered a long wide valley about mid-afternoon and saw at the far end the Corral of the Snakes. Javier had told Lan it got that name because it had been so thick with rattlers one season that it could not be used.

After the camp was set up in a defile beyond the corral, they rode down to look it over. Some of the brush at the wings and

93

walls looked fresh and a new gate had been put up, but there was no cross to show it had been duly consecrated to some saint.

"Perhaps someone made the repairs but found no horses," Blanco said. He leaned from the saddle to examine traces of an old fire. The wind had blown away all evidence of it but the charred ground. "We can't tell from that how long it's been since men camped here, but no one is here now."

After supper, Lan helped Javier unload the cart. He held his breath while he unloaded the partially-tanned hides. Since the bow needed to wait a few days before being worked again, he then started on his arrows, cutting them to the right length and shaping them.

It was a cool, fine night with many stars, and the tragic Corral of the Blessed Saint James seemed far away. Chon played and sang. Lan caught himself knowing many of the words, enough to get the idea of the song.

Love! he thought with a snort. Talking about taking down stars from the sky for a squaw—how crazy could you get?

"Why do you make a rude noise?" frowned Javier. "That is a good song. It is from my home state, Jalisco."

"I don't think a man who would sing it would keep meat in his *tipi* or count many coups."

"I wooed my wife with that song," Javier snapped. "She did not starve, either! *Ay*, that woman! She could polish off half a kid by herself, and enough *frijoles* for six men. Hearty, she was. When she joined the angels I had no heart to marry a lesser woman. She—" Lan interrupted with a raised hand.

"What is that? Horses?"

The faint drumming swelled, then stopped. Javier shrugged. "Horses or wild cattle. Probably spooked by lion scent. Now my wife—"

He was fated not to get to expand on this remarkable woman. Shots rang out of the night. In an instant the mustangers scrambled for shadows, getting out of the dangerous light of the fires. This seemed to confuse the attackers. A few more shots scattered into the area but hit no one.

Blanco shouted a question in Spanish. After a minute a grudging voice replied in another tongue—that of the bluecoats, Lan thought. Inglés jumped up.

Excitedly, though keeping in the dark, he volleyed back in the language. At the answering words, he ran back to the firelight. Down from the opposite rim of the valley came about ten men, all with carbines and rifles.

Their leader, a man with hair as red as Lan's, caught Inglés by the shoulders. They laughed and whacked each other like old friends, still carrying on in that foreign tongue. Then Inglés led the redhead, a brawny, short fellow with a peculiar rolling gait, over to Blanco.

⚑ ⚑ ⚑ *Brother Betrayed*

As Blanco spoke in English with the two men, Lan whispered impatiently to Javier, "Can you understand them?"

"Only a few words. Blanco's not happy, that's plain. The redhead looks as worthless and mean as Inglés. No wonder they're friends!" And Javier spat very close to Inglés' foot.

Inglés talked rapidly, winningly, smiling for once, till Blanco seemed slowly to relax. His eyes were still watchful, though, as he held up his arms and called to his men. Lan understood the gist of the address and Javier supplied the rest from behind the flat of his hand.

The men who had attacked were mustangers under the command of Guero Connors, an old friend of Inglés. *Some commendation!* Lan thought. Several days ago they had repaired this corral and started the run that sent the great herd that panicked into the Corral of the Blessed Saint James. Seeing that the run-together *manadas* were headed in the wrong direction and too many to be turned back, Guero's men had veered off after a smaller group led by a black stallion. They had this manageable troop started for their corral when wildly stampeding horses, remnants of the shambles at Saint James, had scattered them. Guero had especially wanted the fine mares of the black stallion. He had a contract for brood mares with a rancher near Piedras Negras.

And the firing on the camp?

Blanco made a face, but he gave his men Guero's explanation. Guero had thought they were trespassers usurping a corral repaired by his band's labor. Now, however, since he knew this was the organization of the renowned *mesteñero*, Blanco, and his comrade, Inglés, he would like to propose that they throw in together.

Somewhere, not far, were the horses left from the disaster at the other corral, and the black stallion's *manada*. If Guero might claim fifty good mares, Blanco's group could have all the rest. Surely this was a good bargain?

Chon spoke for most of the still-angry mustangers. "Why will you make such an offer, *señor?*"

Blanco translated, though all could see the conciliatory flash of Guero's strong white teeth, hear his deprecating chuckle. His men could not handle the mixed herd and another stampede. Also it was good to see his old friend and visit. And, always, there was the danger of Indians.

This last was a good argument, certainly. Blanco's mustangers murmured, began to nod. When the captain put it to a vote, only Chon and Javier dissented from combining forces, so the agreement was confirmed by a handshake between the two leaders. Lan, of course, had no vote. The new mustangers, all Mexican except for Guero, drifted into camp and were soon playing monte, singing, and acting as if they had always been part of this group instead of the ambushers of it only minutes before.

"I don't like this Guero," Lan muttered to Javier by the cart where they had resumed their work. "I wonder where he knew Inglés?"

"They doubtless were together with Lafitte," Javier hissed. "See? The redhead rolls in his walk like a pirate on a deck!"

Guero, with a cup of Inglés' wretched coffee, was going about the camp at his peculiar gait, acting like a great chief among his inferiors. As he came near Lan, Inglés yelled something that included the word Comanche. Stopping short, Guero glanced at Lan, then broke into hoarse laughter.

Catching hold of Lan's braids, he shouted something he thought very funny. Lan wrested free. Seeing through a fiery haze, ready to leap for the white man's throat, he crouched panting. Then he heard Blanco's voice, speaking English, and Lan blinked to see the captain had come between him and Guero. Inglés, too, had run up, and Blanco, plainly for the benefit of the men, since he had already rebuked Guero, rapped out these words in Spanish.

"All must understand! This boy was raised by Comanches but he is white and he is not a slave. I am responsible for him to the Colonel at the Fort. He is not to be molested."

"He needs the whip," Inglés shot back. "The treacherous whelp'll kill us all some night! I know Indians, I tell you, and—"

"If you fear such a death we can separate." Blanco's hand made a severing motion. His tone was final. "If Connors will not respect my word, he can hunt another corral."

"But he repaired this one!"

"He left it. You know the corrals are free to all unless someone is actually there. One cannot wait about for weeks to make sure a corral is unoccupied." Blanco still used Spanish, probably wishing to make the matter plain to the men.

Inglés gave his broad shoulders a heave. He translated swiftly to Guero, ending with an urgent whisper. Guero's mouth curled. An ugly scar crawled at the roots of his red hair. His eyes burned and froze at once like fire on snow far north, but Blanco coolly returned his gaze.

After a long moment, Guero's snarl bent into a forced grin. He gave his shaggy red head a shake, and turned. But as he swaggered away with Inglés, he gave Lan a murderous stare.

Early next morning the two groups divided into four parties to search for the mustangs. Lan's group came near enough Saint James to see the far circling of cultures. It seemed to Lan that he caught a faint, nauseating stench, but that was impossible at this distance. Marina turned her mare at once and rode over a slope. Lan had heard her crying last night as she fed Diablito. The death of dozens of colts his size in the corral must have been in her mind.

They did not pick up sign of the horses, but when all the men returned to the Corral of the Snakes that night, Chon reported that his party had sighted a vast conglomeration of perhaps three hundred, broken *manadas* and the black stallion's bunch.

"Good!" said Blanco. "In the morning we'll all go after them, except for you and Lázaro, Chon, who must be near the gate if we drive them back suddenly." The mustangers cheered.

It was about time they had some luck. Excitement filled the camp and the holiday fever was raised by a special treat. Inglés had brought in two wild turkeys and Chon had bagged one. These were spitted and supported across a slow fire to baste in their own juices. As Lan collected these best of all arrow feathers, his mouth watered at the succulent odor, but when the mustangers fell upon the rich meat, he produced some jerky.

Inglés, a thigh in one hand and his tin cup in the other, noticed. Face a deep crimson, he came over to Lan and said menacingly, "Too good to eat the turkey I killed, you heathen pup?"

Comanches ate turkey only in extremity. They sensibly knew that animals left their character in their meat. Bear made one brave, deer gave swiftness, buffalo lent strength. But rabbit made even a war chief faint-hearted, and turkey meat would cause him to run away if danger threatened. So, calmly, Lan only told this rude blond, "Turkey gives a coward heart."

"What?" demanded Inglés in strangled fury.

Blanco had heard and moved towards them, chewing on a bone. He understood the turkey ban, of course. Odd, Lan thought, that he still ate it when he had had the privilege of learning better. Blanco said to Inglés, "Do not molest yourself. The boy is not insulting your game. It is just that he has been trained to consider turkey as dangerous."

"Too bad!"

Before Lan could guess his purpose or dodge, Inglés grabbed him, stuffed a mouthful of turkey flesh down his throat. Lan kicked and gagged. The dirty hand in his mouth sickened him even more than the feared meat. He bit down hard as he could, through the turkey, and into Inglés' fingers. He joyed in the sound of teeth hitting bone.

Inglés howled, raised his foot to kick. Blanco jerked him away.

"Stop! Control yourself!"

It seemed the maddened Inglés would rush Blanco to get at Lan. The mustangers drew protectively about their captain. Cursing, Inglés strode over to Guero's group. Blanco, shoulders lax, eyes tired, came to stand by Lan.

"Be careful. You'll get yourself killed."

"Maybe not," Lan said, blood pounding hot in his ears and throat. "I have my knife. And I will have these." He held up the half-formed arrows.

"I have protected you," Blanco said, half to himself. "But I owe Marina to Inglés. Do not force a cruel choice on me, boy."

The camp was up before the sun. Except for Chon, Lázaro, and of course, Javier, all the men swung to their saddles and went north as Chon had directed. In a few hours they picked up the sign of many horses. The dry, hard droppings showed they were weary and under pursuit, lacking time to water and graze. These were horses that had been harassed almost continuously for five to eight days.

Surely this time not even the black could elude his pursuers. If there were, as Chon estimated, about three hundred, that was all the corral could safely hold. Even after Guero took his brood mares there would be a fine drove for Blanco's men.

Impatiently, Lan scanned the monotonous plains till his eyes ached with sun glare. He wanted to get this penning over. Once the herd was delivered to the Fort, they might get after the white Ghost.

Towards noon they sighted the first horses, thrown across the shining rim of the earth. It was as Chon had said. The scrambled *manadas* had made a great circle and were headed in the rough direction of the corral. Blanco and Guero rode close and consulted. Then each signaled his men and the two groups rode widely apart, aiming to come around on either side of the drove once they got behind or to the side of it. The less actual driving they had to do, the better; as long as the mustangs bore south, the men would keep at a distance and press forward only when it became necessary.

Lan squinted at the sun. At this rate they would have the horses penned by dark. A heavy weight seemed to press on his heart, and his tongue grew thick from more than thirst.

What if there were another pile-up? He pushed the dread thought away. These horses should all go in the corral without crowding. They were tired, too fagged for much resistance. Lan was both shamed by this, and glad. For he did not think he could stand another round of killing horses, wind spirits crushed to the ground.

Those men who had *pinole* or jerky chewed as they rode. Marina gave Lan some. Her cheeks were flushed and her hair floated free as a mustang's mane. He thought for the first time that her eyes were the color of a mustang's polished black hoof,

101

then told himself he was so befooled with the Spanish songs of Chon that he was beginning to think that way himself. It was very well for Miguel to watch Marina with the sharp look of jealousy but he, Lan, was not about to think of squaws yet.

They were entering the broad valley that led to the pen. For that day, Lan caught his first glimpse of the black stallion. He ranged far on the other side, nearest Guero's men. And he had not worn down. He drove his *manada* as best he could with all the other horses mingling, slashing at the hind quarters of laggards, whipping recalcitrants into line.

Would he do as he had before? Turn and defy the men? He whirled out of sight and Lan could not see him, strain as he could. If all went well, in minutes now— The corral was less than a hundred yards away. The mustangers began to close in on the flanks and rear.

Shouts came from Guero's side. Trouble? Lan rode along with Blanco and saw why.

The black was up to his old trick, refusing to go further, charging any man who tried to urge him. And the other mustangs, shifting, stopped their steady pace to prison and began to mill behind the stallion; temporarily, at least, he dominated the whole motley drove.

"Yah!" Guero rode in, slapping his rope at the black. It lunged for him. Even at a distance, Lan heard its great teeth click together.

That did it for Guero. He loaded his carbine.

Blanco shouted at him in English, hurrying forward. Guero shrugged, made some blustering reply, but he held his fire while Blanco called up Miguel and Felipe.

"Can you rope that horse?" called the captain.

Miguel laughed confidently. "We'll try." But the stallion had had experience with their ropes and this time they could not catch him, cast their loops cunningly as they might. Guero muttered. Blanco gave him a grim look.

"My captain," said Inglés with startling courtesy, "let me crease him. Otherwise, as you see, he must be destroyed before he loses us the herd."

"I want him for my own," Blanco said. He sighed, studied the nervous mustangs that any whiff of breeze might stampede. "All right. But aim carefully."

Lan knew about creasing. Braves who had rifles tried it sometimes when they despaired of getting a horse any other way. It meant to shoot so skillfully that the bullet hit the muscular part of the neck above the horse's spine so it would be stunned for a few minutes. There was tiny room for error. A fraction too low and the horse died.

"Wait!" Lan hardly knew he had spoken till he had. "Let me try to talk to him."

"Talk?" Blanco demanded. "Are you mad?"

"I—I can often tame horses that way. It is a gift. I don't know how I do it, but I can."

Blanco frowned. "And you didn't intend, ever, to tell me of this talent?"

"No," Lan muttered, hanging his head.

"You thought you would do only what you had to? Nothing extra?"

Blanco had been good to him. Lan's cheeks were hot as he nodded. He squared his shoulders, looking the white-haired captain in the eyes. "But now I tell you. You want the stallion alive. Let me try!"

The lips beneath the black moustache pulled down. "Well, if you think you can. But if he attacks you, we'll bring him down."

"Stay back unless he does," Lan advised. "He's strung-up and won't let me close unless you all move away." In his excitement, Lan had spoken in Comanche. Blanco had to translate to the others who reacted according to their feelings for Lan. Chon and Miguel looked worried, Marina started to protest. But Inglés and Guero laughed.

Maybe they had reason. Lan could not be sure his voice would always work. And he had never, certainly, tried it under such bad conditions. The mustangers drew back, leaving him to face the black.

Lan's heart tripped fast. His mouth was dry as an old leaf, his tongue as brittle. This stallion was a veritable marvel of strength and will to have kept his *manada* going this long. Every fiber of him, each nerve, hated man. Could the horse-talk work with him? Lan took a slow breath, tasting it.

If he failed he would most likely be killed. At least he did not need to worry about humiliation. The worst would be that his failure meant the death of the black, too. To save it, Lan had to call its secret sound, whisper in the way that would master and calm.

Closing his eyes, Lan lifted his face to the fading sun warmth. He prayed silently. *Great Spirit, I have no medicine. But You put the voice in me to tame horses. Strengthen it now.* Feeling better, Lan put everything from his mind but the black horse and stepped forward.

He sniffed. He became a horse, a strange master mustang, peering around at the men, scenting the breeze. Like a visitor sure of his welcome, he came near the black.

Puzzled, the stallion watched, pawed experimentally. He snorted almost in question.

"Hua," Lan said softly. "Hua, hua, hua—" The black laid back its ears, but Lan came up to it gently, confidently. The magic voice was in Lan and he was not himself but a horse and he knew what to do as if he watched himself approach from lowered mustang eyes. "Hua. Hua . . ."

Brother, brother. Before the earth we were; before shape we were. I know your name, I call it, it is the sound. You know me. You know the sound put in us by the Great Spirit. It is be-

tween us and I know you. This is your sound. Brother. Brother.

Beside the black, touching muscled, quivering flesh, whispering in the ear. Softly, softly. A shudder ran through the horse. He moved restively.

"Hua, hua . . ."

Lan ran his hands over the stallion who trembled but stood still, flaked dried lather from its neck, patted dust from rump and withers. Then, talking constantly, Lan turned. With his hand in its mane, he walked the stallion around the fringe of horses, into the brush wings. The black moved as if drugged, pulled by the voice. Lan got him into the corral as the other horses, following, crowded in.

The black, rousing for the first time, went stiff, shied violently from the walls. Lan felt like a traitor.

"This way you are not dead," he cried, as if the horse could understand. The human words, realization of the trap, shocked the stallion out of his docility. He raged up, striking at Lan. The mustangs were packing in. Lan slipped behind one and vaulted on its back, went up on his feet, and over the pickets of the corral.

Scratched, knocked breathless, he lay on his hands and knees outside the corral while the herd thundered in. He could still hear the stallion squealing in frenzy. Lan lay on his face, trembled, was sick.

When he finally dragged himself to the wings, the catch was finished. Chon and Lázaro had shut the gate. The men were whooping, shouting. At sight of Lan, they called, "Bravo." Lan stumbled away.

He had called the black horse Brother, made it true—and betrayed him. No good to remind himself that the horse would otherwise have almost surely died. The screams of the trapped animals rang in his head. He came to the edge of the arroyo, had to stop there, clenching and unclenching his hands. He did not know what else he could have done, yet he felt wrong, condemned, treacherous.

Great Spirit . . .

What? What would he ask now, the white Comanche of no medicine? That one thing he had, the horse-talk, weighed on him like a corpse, like the broken mustangs at Saint James, the ones that would die here before they were tamed. He could trap wild things. That was his gift! He squeezed his eyes shut.

Something soft rubbed his arm. Lan jumped. He must have been standing there a long time for now it was dark. But he could make out Diablito by his elbow. And there was Marina. She held out a bowl. Lan shook his head.

"Yes!" She thrust the dish into his hands. "Eat, or I'll feed you like Diablito. See, he wants you to eat, too. He does not want his friend to grow weak."

She really would feed him, or try to, Lan knew. Half-heartedly, he dipped into the bowl with the spoon she produced. The stew tasted spicy and good, warming to his sick stomach. Before he knew it, the bowl was empty. Marina sat down, hugging her knees, and Diablito hung near them in the warm night.

"What you did," Marina said at last. "It was brave. Valiant."

Lan choked. "It was a traitor's trick!" He put down the bowl and left her.

✄ ✄ ✄ *Lost Voice*

Now came the worst part of mustanging, waiting for the horses to become subdued by thirst and hunger till they could be driven to the Fort. There was no water in the pen and no way to feed them so it was necessarily cruel. For Lan, the only relieving fact was that these mustangs, already tired and thirsty, would not have to be confined long.

"Sometimes we must keep them penned six days," Blanco said. "We will try taking these out in two. We'll clog any obstreperous ones, but I hope most can be herded by just the help of the bell mares and mules."

During the two days, Lan put his arrows away to season and worked his bow, rubbing it till it had a polished sheen. Javier had a glue stick, such as was used by Comanches, and he loaned this to Lan. This glue was made of horns and hoofs boiled in water. Cooled on a smooth stick, it could be conveniently carried and softened in hot water when needed. Lan did this now and spread the smelly substance over the bow. Then he wet the sinew he had saved from the deer and wrapped this around the wood. Another coat of glue was thoroughly rubbed in on the sinew. When this dried the constricted sinew would shrink close to the wood and with the hardened glue form a very tough, durable bow.

Lan put the bow to dry on the cart. He felt sorry to have

done with it for the corral haunted him, and the thought of the black stallion there. Javier caught him staring down at the pen, touched his shoulder with rough kindness.

"Blanco will treat the black well, lad."

Lan nodded. But he remembered, with bitterness in his mouth, a saying of Arrow In His Shield: *The best master weighs more than a mountain.* It was so for him, a human, used to some restraints; how could it be for a wild stallion with the speed and will of the wind?

The men watched Lan with respect that would have flattered him once but stung like salt in a wound because of the circumstances. In his guilt, he felt no tinge of glory. People, both white and Comanche, had never felt him one of them. Only horses had known him. And this was how he used their trust.

It was noon the second day when Blanco lounged over. He made Javier a cigarette, commented on Lan's bow, and finally spoke in Comanche.

"I see your face. You are sick in your heart. Is it for the stallion?"

"That is done," Lan said, surveying the ground.

Blanco sat down as if for a companionable chat. "I have heard of horse-whisperers but I did not believe. That is a great power, boy."

"Great evil—used as I did."

Blanco's thick brows climbed towards his white hair. "It would be better if Inglés had creased the black, likely killed it?"

Lan kept still. He wished Blanco would go away. He had gone over this incessantly. It did no good! If he had not—but he had— There was no way he could be right. He didn't blame Blanco. The captain only pursued his living. But he, Lan, had taken a gift and used it against what he loved. Blanco got to his feet.

"One thing." His voice sounded weary, discouraged. "When the mustangs are delivered, we will hunt the Ghost. I had meant to turn you white again, bring you back to your blood people. Now I will not hold you longer than I must to keep my word to the colonel."

Work on the bow completed, Lan could not fight a compulsion that had been growing on him. He had to see if the black lived, know if, in the morning, the stallion would be one of the horses that came out of the pen.

Leaving camp as unobtrusively as he could, Lan made his way slowly around the corral, peering in through the brush and pickets. There was such a concentrated stench of sweat, manure, and decay that his stomach churned uneasily.

Bay, black, dun, pinto, gray—all colors were packed in the enclosure. When he was about to give up, Lan saw the proud head of the black stallion raised above the press. He was near enough that Lan could see the glaze on his eyes, the way he seemed to weave as if asleep on his feet.

"Hua . . ." Lan whispered, scarcely knowing he did so.

The dull eyes alerted. Peeling his lips back over yellow teeth, the stallion squealed in rage. That voice would never tame him again.

In fact— Suddenly cold to the heart, Lan whispered once more. It did not take the frenzy of the black to confirm his dread.

Lan's voice would not calm any horse. It was just common, human sound, not the key tone of horse-talk, that secret vibration. *I've lost it*, Lan thought. *It's gone.* Though it had been lately a curse, he felt stripped, totally bereft of identity. If he had wondered who he was, where he belonged before, what could he think now?

He was no Comanche. He had no medicine power. His parents, beloved as they were, were not his flesh forebears. Now he had not even that inborn voice. He was somebody called

Lan, because even a slave was called something for the convenience of its owners. Once he did gain freedom, he had no place to go. He would not, could not, be Swift Otter's son forever, tolerated for her sake.

Then he saw a jeering face, heard a taunt from almost a moon past, and knew he had one reason to live, at least, one thing to do. He would have vengeance on Yellow Wolf. And that was enough to think on now, enough reason to bear whatever came and to chase the white Ghost.

As he came from the pen, a husky voice hailed him in Spanish. It was Inglés, strolling with Guero. They had a blanket and Guero held something in his hand.

"Want to see some fun, boy?" Inglés invited. "We're going to race fleas."

Lan had seen the mustangers do this. They used variations, but mainly it consisted of marking a goal and seeing which of several fleas could get there first. He shook his head.

"I must help Javier."

"That was good work with the stallion." Inglés' smile looked painful, as if a tooth were being pulled, but he sounded hearty. "What bunch of Indians did you run with?"

"The band of Thunder Waters of the Wasps."

"They teach you that horse-talk?"

Again Lan shook his head. He walked off before they could pry any further. Strange. He had been lonely all his life. Now when he wanted to be left alone, all men called to him. But that would stop if they knew the truth. That he had lost his voice.

As Lan dropped by Javier and began wordlessly to help sort hair, he sensed the old man's curiosity and decided to speak first, divert attention from his trip to the corral.

"This Guero—his men are Mexican. Why does he not speak their language?"

Javier grunted. "Him! To begin, he is stupid as a brush-hog. Add to that his conviction that all languages but his own are barbaric and you have it." Blanco had joined them while they talked. Now he laughed.

"You speak of the fire-topped one. I asked him the same question. He replied that he could swear in Spanish horribly enough to get across to his men they would have to learn English. Enough to comprehend him. From what I have seen he relies on kicks and loudness more than words anyhow." He looked at Lan. "You were at the corral. Was anything amiss?"

"There is a smell of death."

"Some die of indignation," Blanco said. He glanced at Diablito who had come up to butt against Lan's arm. "That little fellow is happy. He will grow up tame as a puppy raised under a bed. But older mustangs—some cannot live as captives. They have a need for freedom strong as a need for food. These die before they are broken."

"Will the black be one of those?"

"*Quién sabe?*" Blanco considered Lan a moment. "Perhaps you would talk to him again."

"No!"

To the amazed stares fixed on him, Lan spoke more quietly, but with conviction. "It would do no good. He will not trust that voice again." Blanco did not argue, though a muscle jerked in his cheek.

"You are obligated to help me, but not to use your special power." Finishing his cigarette, he walked away.

"That was ill spoken." Javier's tone was reproachful. "Blanco has been kind to you."

Lan had not meant to tell what had happened, but, maddened at the old man's rebuke, he blazed forth, "I do not have the voice! It left me. And," he added fiercely, "I am glad it has. I can betray no more wild ones by calling them brother."

111

Red sundown painted the corral like blood. When the gate was opened tomorrow how many horses would be dead?

The men saddled and gathered their possessions after early breakfast and the bell mares and mules were brought up to the wings of the corral and clogs were brought to impede the wilder mustangs. These clogs were forked sticks which would be lashed to a front ankle. Guero's band waited with ropes to catch their share. They would be driving due south instead of southeast, so this marked the ending of the alliance.

Inglés rode up to Blanco. "Guero feels he should have a hundred mares instead of fifty," said the blond, looking everywhere but at the captain. "We made a big catch and you will still have the big share."

Blanco stiffened. His eyes narrowed. Then, obviously controlling his feelings, he said briefly, "Cut them out."

"But he claimed only fifty mares," Miguel protested.

"When you have made a bargain with a man of bad faith," said Blanco, "the sooner you part from him the better, even at a cost."

Guero tugged at Inglés, laughed when his friend explained what Blanco had said, and chortled out a retort which brought a frown to Blanco who disdained to answer in English.

"We won't quarrel over a few mustangs, no." The captain used Spanish, slowly, deliberately, so both bands of men understood. "I will just shoot Connors if he comes to me with any new bargains. Tell him that, Inglés."

Turning, the mustanger chief called to Chon to open the gate. At first the benumbed horses stayed quiet. Then they saw the bell mares and mules. In a few seconds the wild horses were following the tame lead animals down to the water.

At its blessed scent, the mustangs raised their heads. Nostrils quivering, they made for the hole. Lan watched with a slackening of tension almost as great as if he, like them, were quenching a long thirst after days without water.

Some dazed, some jittery, out came the mustangs from the pen. The colts, having suckled, were in better shape than Lan had hoped, but they still lagged and teetered as if their knobby legs might crumble. Guero's men had stationed themselves on either side of the water hole. When they saw a fine mare come up from drinking, they roped her. The other horses fell in with the bell mares and mules except for a few that tried to bolt. Blanco's mustangers caught these and applied clogs, lashing the prongs of the forked sticks together in front of the ankle. The horses quickly found that anything faster than a walk would make the hind foot catch on the stick and cause tripping besides a painful skinning of the ankle.

The last horse out was the black stallion. He came at a gallop, lured by freedom, ready to assert his power. Before he could reach the herd, Blanco and Miguel roped him. While he lay pinioned, Chon quickly tied one end of a short rope about the fetlock joint and the other around the black's neck. When the stallion was let up, he had to go on three legs which, of course, effectively slowed him. Blanco used this method instead of a clog to keep from scarring him.

Caught by motion behind the stallion, Lan gazed down by the water hole. Why, Guero's men were holding down their mares and—yes, they had out knives!

"Blanco!" Lan cried, pointing as he rode forward. Blanco saw immediately.

"Wait!" he shouted. He sent his mount flying down the arroyo. When he pulled in by the startled men, his carbine was out.

Guero stood up, wiping blood off his knife and hands on his shirt. The mare he had knelt by struggled up, her knee ligament cut. She would be lame forever. Like Javier, to whom Comanches had done the same thing.

Eyes gleaming, Guero jerked out a question in English. Blanco answered in a tightly furious voice. The other men thought it best to let up the other as yet "unkneed" mares. Inglés rode over.

"Now, Blanco, those are Guero's mustangs. He doesn't want to fool with chasing strays all the way to Piedras Negras. The mares can still raise colts. That's what they're wanted for."

Blanco's lips were white. "I will not let him do that to a hundred mares! Or to one more. They will never run again!"

"You don't have it in mind to cheat my friend out of his catch?"

Hand on his carbine tightening, Blanco used carefully spaced words. "I would kill you for that had you not restored Marina. As it is, I count us even. If your fine *camarada* cannot get these mares to his buyer without maiming, tell him I will buy them here."

"You have the gold?" asked Inglés in surprise.

"No. I will pay at the Fort after the horses are sold."

Inglés spat disgustedly. He translated to Guero who looked dismayed, then surly. He growled something, eyeing Blanco warily. Blanco laughed, spoke in Spanish for the men's benefit.

"So—Guero deserted during the Mexican War. That is why he won't go near a Fort!" Inglés passed this on to Guero who, after a flash of anger, grinned evilly, and replied in English. Javier, who had come up, whispered the meaning to Lan.

"Guero says the United States whipped the Mexicans without him, so it worked out all right. He says if Blanco can't pay now he'll knee the mares and go on to Piedras Negras."

Blanco answered in English, but his loading the carbine showed the content of his words to everyone. Inglés spoke hastily to Guero. After some argument, he looked questioningly at Blanco who spoke grimly.

"Put Guero's words into Spanish. I want all our men to hear.

114

Their work gives them a share in the horses." Inglés shrugged and obeyed.

"If you will let one of his men come with you to the Fort to fetch back the sale money, Guero agrees to sell you the mares."

"He may send his man. Since some horses may die on the way and I have the risk of the drive and the labor, I will pay him four dollars a head for the hundred. The colonel pays me five, so that is fair."

This was put into English for Guero who nodded with surprising affability. His men took their ropes off the horses which then swarmed after the moving herd. Blanco's men caught and clogged the few unruly ones. Blanco looked at Inglés. It was plain that the captain was torn between his debt to this man and anger at his behavior.

"Do you ride with us, Inglés?"

Inglés shook his head. "No hard feelings. But having met my old pard again, I guess I'll stay with him."

"Adiós, then." Blanco reined his horse after the mustangs. Javier climbed back in his cart, whipped up the mules. Even the unwieldy cart traveled faster than the one lamed mare who hobbled last. Lan was glad when a colt, evidently hers, ranged back from the main drove to stay beside her. Guero's representative fell into herding position. Diablito, according to his fancy, chased Lan or Marina, or trotted by the cart.

It was good to have the horses unpenned, to start on the last part of this enterprise. Lan had taken only one quick glance into the corral. Perhaps a dozen mustangs lay dead there. How many died from lack of water, how many from lack of freedom, there was no way to guess.

Even in the open, there were cruel sights. The clogged horses, the hobbled black stallion moving with his haughty crest pulled low by the weight of his bound foreleg. And the hamstrung mare.

"Listen," said Javier as Lan watched her. "She'll heal and enjoy good grass. Life almost any way is sweet. I know."

"For the stallion, too?" Lan jerked his head towards the pitifully hampered leader.

"Yes, even for him. Blanco will probably put him on his ranch to herd a *manada* and sire fine colts. He may not ever ride him. I tell you, Blanco loves the wild ones though it is his only way of life, bringing them in."

Lan did not argue with his older friend. But he knew that however unmolested a man or horse might live, there was a difference in being owned and being free.

Since the mustangs could not go faster than a walk, the progress was slow. They camped fairly early that night because this was the only close water, got an early start next day, and reached the Rio Grande by night. Blanco said it was three more days to the Fort.

As they had done the night before, half the men stayed up to night-herd while the others slept. Lan had the first watch. He settled at one side of the herd and soon was half-drowsing from weariness and the lulling hum of insects. Diablito had sprawled down beside him, so Lan tried to stay alert by talking to the little fellow. Diablito did not mind that the horse-talk had deserted Lan.

A shifting of sand warned Lan of movement behind him. He turned to see a looming figure that came close and assumed identity in the dim light of the new moon. It was Guero's man, a stocky moustached person with one finger missing, probably from getting it caught between the saddle horn and his "dallied" rope. Lan stared at the unmistakable shape of a holstered pistol at the man's side.

Squatting down by Lan, the man offered tobacco. Lan refused. He had only smoked from Comanche pipes, usually in a ceremonial way, and he felt that smoking was a semi-religious rite not to be shared with just anybody.

"A dull night," said the man. "Not even the mustangs are restless."

"That is good," Lan said. He wished his visitor would go away.

"You've learned Spanish pretty well, boy. Your Indian folks going to like that?"

"So long as I come back safely, my mother will not care."

"Will she be as broad-minded about your being a servant?"

Lan bit back his anger. A fool's chatter should bother no one. He said, "I will soon go back to my people."

"Ah," said the stranger, leaning forward, the garlic on his breath filling the air. "Why don't you go back *now?*"

✒ ✒ ✒ *Night Raid*

"I must stay with Blanco till we catch the white Ghost," Lan said. "That's why."

The shoulders of the dark shape moved carelessly. "What is a promise given under threats? You aren't going to get a share of the profits on this herd?"

"No."

"There you are!" The man's voice warmed confidingly. "You're being cheated just like Guero said. And after the way you toned down that stallion! Use your brain, lad. Why should you work for this cheap bunch and get nothing from it?"

Lan frowned. "Say what you mean."

"Gladly! Guero's camped up the arroyo, close enough to see a fire from here. He's let Blanco drive to the Rio for him. Now he'll take over as soon as he sees my signal fire. He told me to offer you this deal. Help us run off the herd and when we sell, you'll get a full share."

"He's going to take all the horses? Not just his mares?"

"Why take some when he can have all?"

Deciding he had better find out all about this, Lan asked, "Why am I worth so much to him?"

"You can horse-talk. You could go in pastures and bring out the best stallions, without any fuss. Guero wants you for a partner. You'd be your own boss and earn a nice pile of money. What more could you ask for, and you only a kid?"

"Where are we to build the fire?"

The man laughed. "That's it! I thought you were clever." He rose, pointing northwest. "I'm to make the fire right over the hill, let it burn a few minutes. Guero will be here in half-an-hour. This camp won't know what—" So wrapped up was the spy in his anticipation that he did not notice Lan's hand creep to his gun-belt.

Making the last motion in a flash, Lan swung out the pistol, brought it crashing down on the man's head. The man dropped like a weighted bag. Lan ran for Blanco, shook the captain awake, and poured out the danger.

"Let's make sure our friend doesn't get away," Blanco said, springing up. Hurrying to the edge of the herd, they bound the unconscious spy. Lan looked worriedly at Blanco who rubbed his moustache.

"Mmm. Well, they're expecting a fire. We won't disappoint them."

"What?"

"I've had enough trouble with that crew. It's time they shared it. Light the fire, Lan, right where it's expected." Blanco added as if to himself, "Inglés helped plan this. He knew the route I'd take, where I'd camp. Why must he make me forget a sacred debt?"

Lan gathered loose brush and grass, started a fire with the flint and steel he always carried. As the man had indicated, Lan threw dust over the blaze after it had leaped high for several minutes. He got back to camp to find the mustangers saddling.

Javier, Marina, and a few men were left to watch the horses. The rest of the band rode back the way they had come that day. The few rifles were augmented by knives and machetes, and all the men had ropes.

They filed down into the arroyo which Guero's group must cross, dismounted, and took positions at the crossing. "Now," said Blanco, grim satisfaction in his voice, "we are ready to welcome our guests."

Hoofbeats drummed softly like a ghost herd coming. Knowing there would be night-herders, Guero would come as quietly as he could. Lan waited tensely as the horses neared. The first started his downward climb. Two, three—four—eight—ten. That was all!

"*Bueno!*" Blanco rose from a ledge, his carbine glinting. "We have you surrounded. Put high your hands."

Consternation poured from the thieves in two languages. Inglés growled, "The Comanche brat! He told. I said not to trust him!" And he seemed to take savage pleasure in repeating this in English to his cursing partner. Blanco gave them a minute to vent their anger and then spoke in a pleasant tone.

"I will make you a business proposition. Some of the horses were yours—not all, but some. Will you trade them for your lives?"

As Inglés put this into English for Guero, Blanco went on. "It is true, as I see you are about to say, that the mares are worth far more than you. But you should be prejudiced. Decide quickly. We have lost quite enough sleep for you this night."

"You've got us," Inglés gritted. "Let us go. You can keep the horses."

"That is sensible of you," Blanco approved. "But I cannot turn you loose to come down and cause more trouble."

"What will you do?" Panic flared in Inglés' query. "You promised—"

"Have no anxiety. Tomorrow you'll go free as birds—vultures." Blanco gave commands. His men roughly got the thieves from their saddles, disarmed them, and roped their hands. They were herded up the arroyo.

There on the slope, Blanco had their feet bound, too. Two men were left on guard and the rest went back to camp for such sleep as might be had before morning. Exhausted as he was from standing first watch and the interception of the rogue mustangers, Lan had a hard time getting to sleep. Inglés and Guero had watched him while their feet were bound in a way that said they would never forget him.

Before dawn next day, Blanco ordered the herd out. Only Lan stayed with him when the leader rode down to send the night guards after the horses. Between Blanco and Lan rode the spy, bound in the saddle.

At the top of the slope, Blanco dumped a blanket on the ground. It held the knives, rifles, pistols, and machetes of Guero's crew. Lan wondered mightily but held back his questions. Blanco did not look like a man to be bothered with questions that morning.

After the guards were on their way, Blanco yanked the spy to the ground near Guero and tied his feet. Without a word, Blanco remounted, started to ride away.

"Wait!" Inglés shouted, twisting vainly to sit up. "You aren't going to leave us like this?"

Blanco turned. "At the top of the small hill are your weapons. You can reach them, crawling, in about two hours. It will not take you too long, I think, to cut loose your ropes."

"You could at least turn us free long enough to cook some breakfast and get a drink," wheedled the blond.

"You'll have plenty of time to do that later." Blanco grinned. "In spite of your promise, I prefer distance between us."

"You mean you're just going to let us bake here in the sun and wriggle up that hill on our bellies—like snakes?"

Blanco nodded cheerfully. "It distresses me much more to pen wild horses without water."

"Where are our horses?"

"I sent them on with the herd." At the storm of invective, Blanco added smoothly, "Your saddles and packs are at our camp site, so you will not go hungry, and the whole Rio is near for your thirst. I cannot leave horses. You might pursue and annoy us. But it will not take cunning fellows like you long to catch new mounts. And here," Blanco tossed down a pouch that clinked, "are five dollars apiece for each horse."

Lan and Blanco started off. As if in afterthought, Blanco turned. "When you do get loose and collect your gear, you would be wise to keep going in another direction. I am sending a message ahead to the colonel, telling him of our trouble, and if I'm not there soon with the herd, he'll know whom to come after."

"This won't be the last of us," Inglés yelled, dragging himself to his elbows, trying to shake his pinioned fist. "You, Comanche brat, I'll make you sorry you ever saw daylight!"

"Your talk is worthless as you are," Blanco said. "*Vamos,* Lan."

As they rode up the slope, Lan could feel hating eyes bore into his back. He despised Inglés and Guero, but he was afraid of them and could not help saying to Blanco, "That pair will get even or die trying."

"It is possible." Blanco sighed, then stiffened his spine. "One thing about it. I no longer owe Inglés anything. If they had raided our camp, some of my men would have died, maybe even my daughter. Should he bother us again, I will not give him his life."

Riding at a swift pace, they caught up with the herd about noon. "I do not expect a chase," the captain said. "However, to be safe—" He called Chon and sent him ahead with a report to the colonel. Chon would get there by nightfall, but it would take the clogged mustangs another day.

Lan watched them, a bitter taste in his mouth. The black stallion hobbled along, his head bent level with that of the kneed mare who dragged miserably at the rear.

"You do not like that." It was Blanco, beside him.

Unable to speak, Lan shook his head. They rode in silence for a time. Blanco chewed the edge of his moustache ferociously. At last he said, "Listen, boy. I am twice in your debt. I cannot let you go till we catch the colonel's stallion, but—for you—I will release the black."

Lan stared, dumbfounded. Blanco raised his hand to show he wanted no interruptions. "Had you not warned me of the spy, we would have lost the herd and probably our lives. I cannot let the black go till the other horses are safely penned or he might stampede them. You and I will hold him back when we get within a few miles of the Fort. Then, when the mustangs are out of trouble range, we'll let him loose."

Inside, Lan felt a glow like the sun. He had lost his one gift, but at least the animal he had betrayed with it would go free. Back to gather other mares and sire fine colts. Back to remember the humbling rope only the better to elude it.

Night camp, with guards, was uneventful. They followed the Rio now, and by late afternoon passed the dry river bed down which Lan had come with Yellow Wolf nearly a moon ago. Here Blanco put Lázaro in charge of the herd. Lan helped the captain cut the black stallion out of the stragglers, but his scent so provoked the mustang that when this was done, Lan retired to a distance. Blanco fastened the lassoed stallion to a mesquite and rode over to Lan.

"We might as well climb off. It'll be an hour before we can untie him. *Ay*, horses!"

Settling to the earth, Lan said, "My father told me that one time we did not have the horse. Dogs hauled our belongings and we *walked!*" He laughed. "Imagine, The People, on foot! Father said that when we first had horses we called them the God-dogs because they could carry so much more than dogs."

"It is true, once there were no horses here," Blanco said seriously. He pushed back his sombrero and rolled a cigarette, plainly enjoying this luxury of a talk during work time. "Our priest who has studied such things says that the wild ones started with a colt foaled by a brown mare aboard a ship of Cortez. Cortez had sixteen horses. They had a hard time traveling in the ice and snow of the mountains and the colt was lost or abandoned somewhere near Orizaba. Later, Indians saw a white colt running with deer on the mountain. He was the first mustang. When Oñate led colonists to New Mexico in 1596, he lost hundreds of horses and mules. And so it went. Spaniards lost their horses and the country gained them."

"I did not know all that," said Lan, upping Spaniards several notches in his esteem. How terrible if they had never brought horses! The Comanches would still be trailing around behind dogs! Lan tried to picture this country without horses and could not. They belonged to mesquite, the wind, the sun. Dizzied at the effort, Lan came back to the present. "Are you mustangers subject to laws, to the blue-coats or the Mexicans?"

Blanco smiled. "Well, there are laws. Spain and later Mexico claimed the wild horses and cattle as government property and charged a tax on each one captured. Hunters of them were to get a license of the nearest *alcalde*, an official, and run the wild ones only from October to March. Few mustangers bothered. What did the *alcalde*, fat and safe in his town, know of our life? He did not protect us. We ran all the risk and felt we deserved all the profit. Then Texas became a republic, and later, part of the United States. There are still laws and no protection, so nothing has changed."

Lan could not argue. He thought the white man's law difficult to understand, anyway. Clearly a wild horse belonged to whoever caught it. Blanco explained further. "Honest *mesteñeros* do not gather herds on land where someone runs private *manadas*. It would result in stealing."

"You mean a man can claim land for his own? Keep others off it?"

"He can try, and does," Blanco laughed.

"That is bad," Lan judged, frowning. "The earth is for all—The People," he added quickly.

"There you spoke like a true Comanche—or Texan, Spaniard, or Mexican! Do you not know, boy, that all races consider *themselves* The People?"

"At least," retorted Lan, "Comanches do not take land for themselves as a private possession. All use it for hunting, camping, whatever is desired. We own horses, tents, clothing, weapons, those things. But we would not claim land more than we would try to catch sunlight, air, or water, and call it one man's."

Shrugging, Blanco said, "White men own land as an Indian owns his horse. And he'll fight just as hard for it."

Lan screwed up his face, trying to imagine the earth divided into parcels and a man on each small part fighting off everybody else. Why, how could such people get anything done? And how could they hunt on their little plots, or do much but raise crops like squaws? As if reading his mind, Blanco continued.

"I would say that at least half the white man's battles, both private and national, are over land. The United States and Mexico disputed their boundaries for years. When the Texans defeated Santa Anna in 1836, many Mexican ranchers fled south of the Rio, leaving their land and cattle. My uncle did this, and still hasn't regained his land or the fair price guaranteed for such property under the Treaty of Guadalupe Hidalgo. This treaty, made after the United States won its war with Mexico in 1847, offered citizenship to those Mexicans who wished to remain within the new limits of the United States and agreed to pay for the lands of those who preferred to move to Mexico."

"There has been all this between your people and the blue-coats. Yet you supply them with horses!"

"A grudge carried long is a bone stuck in the throat. Why should I choke over what happened twenty years ago? My uncle has a new ranch and enjoys railing against the gringos." Blanco glanced at the waning sun and got to his feet. "We can let the black go now."

"You had better do it," Lan said. "My smell maddens him."

Swiftly, Blanco removed the rope from the fetlock and neck. Before the stallion comprehended his freedom, the mustanger had his *reata* off the tree and the black, and was vaulting to the saddle.

"Ride!" called Blanco. For the stallion, coming to himself, tossing his head, was snorting and eyeing his recent captors. Lan nudged Friend after the captain.

Glancing back, he saw the black sniff, picking up the scent of the herd. But Lan and Blanco were going that way, and the stallion had had all the men he wanted. The last Lan saw of him, he had lain down to roll and stretch. Soon the stiffness would leave his muscles. He would regain his strength. And then stallions with mares would have to look out!

"I give him a month," Blanco said, "to have as big a *manada* as ever. And he knows about men now. I doubt he can ever be caught."

The two of them rode leisurely the few miles to the Fort. The lights, even to Lan, had a friendly look. "We will be here a week or more," Blanco said. "We gentle the horses for the colonel and thus double the price we get. And in the morning we will hold the *lazo de las ánimas*."

"What is that?" Lan puzzled.

"All proper mustangers catch out a *lazo*—two horses from herds of over a hundred. The *lazo* is sold to pay for prayers for the souls of dead *mesteñeros*. Since we have such a big herd, I will dedicate four mustangs for this purpose."

"Yet you said you had no law."

"This is custom," said Blanco. "And respect."

Lan hushed. That was the Comanche attitude. Though they had little actual law, their customs were strong and few men cared to do anything that would make them looked down on among The People. Public opinion and tradition were the strongest controllers of behavior.

As they neared the corrals, two figures came running out to meet them. Miguel and Marina, as their voices proved before the newcomers were close enough to see them distinctly.

"Lan," called Marina, "the colonel asked many questions about you! There is a priest here from Brownsville, also curious. Father, you won't send Lan back with him, will you?"

"How you clatter!" said Blanco. The surprise in his tone wiped out Lan's first startled suspicion of double-dealing, some plan to send him to the white men. "The colonel and I made an agreement. He will keep his word. Lan will not go with any priest unless he wishes."

"Anyway," announced Miguel, "the colonel asks you to report as soon as you have eaten, and bring Lan. Hurry to camp! Javier bought wonderful tortillas and *gorditos* from a laundress. And she promises to supply us fresh each day. *Ay*, such food!"

Blanco lifted his reins. "I must put you to breaking horses in the morning before you turn complete glutton," he said with mock severity. "You had better have left me some *gorditos*, those nice fat little rolls, or I'll send you to the laundress for more!"

Taking his daughter up before him, Blanco rode into the

mustangers' camp, dismounted near the cart. He received Chon's report while Lan and Miguel attended to the horses. Diablito's nuzzling at Lan could not allay the worry crowding him. As the two boys came back to the fire, Lan asked, "You are sure the priest inquired for me?"

"Positive," said Miguel. He touched Lan's shoulder. "Don't worry, *amigo*. My godfather will not give you up to the civilized ones. Come sit and enjoy this feast! I've had some, but I'll join you for courtesy's sake!"

"Courtesy, nothing," growled Javier, filling Lan a heaping bowl. "You may eat a tortilla, Miguel the Monkey! Or go twirl your rope!" But he relented and gave Miguel a hot *gordito* smeared with honey.

There were small kernels cooked with dried currants, a rich stew of what Marina said was mutton. She told Lan the kernels were rice. In spite of his worry over the priest, Lan ate ravenously. He thought it almost better than fresh liver cooked on coals and spread with marrow. Diablito came up to push at Marina. She laughed and petted him.

"He had a feast, too," she explained. "One of the officers keeps a cow to furnish milk for his children, and he gave me some for this small mischief!"

The whole camp radiated an air of contentment and satisfaction. They had brought in a fine large herd, presently housed in the largest corral, defeated Inglés' treachery, and had broken their monotonous camp diet. The mustangs, supplied with water and feed, could be gentled without undue brutality. Forgotten were the bitter chases, the dead mustangs at Saint James. Children and a few older people had come from the Fort to visit or watch. Games of chance and singing had already begun when Blanco wiped his mouth, sighed, and rose as sluggishly as was possible for him.

"Come, Lan. We will go to the colonel."

As they neared the headquarters, Lan's feet grew heavy with dread. It seemed a lifetime had passed since he crept along here with Yellow Wolf. Surely he would not have to go with the priest?

"You—you say a priest is like a shaman?" Lan asked, swallowing hard.

"In some ways. He is respected because he serves the Great Spirit and speaks for Him."

"Then will the colonel not do as he says?"

Blanco looked at Lan. "Listen, don't worry. You will not have to do anything beyond your bargain."

⚜ ⚜ ⚜ *White Blood Calling*

The robed priest was young with fair hair and blue eyes. He turned from speaking with the colonel and greeted Blanco and Lan. He spoke Spanish with a winning, inquiring accent and watched Lan so probingly that Lan dug his moccasined toe in the dirt floor and wished himself a hundred miles away.

Blanco and the colonel spoke briefly in English. Blanco glanced uneasily at the priest, but he took the cigar the colonel offered and sat down, leaving Lan to face the visitor.

"I am Father Denis of the Brownsville Oblates," began the young man, smiling as if to put Lan at ease. "A letter has come to us from Scotland by way of London and our home office in France—a long route. Knowing that the Oblates travel like missionaries along the Rio Grande, a family in Scotland is trying to find a certain Alan Graeme who came this way twelve years ago. They have learned that Graeme with his wife and three children booked passage from New Orleans to Point Isabel near Brownsville. Graeme lived in Brownsville some months. He became well-known for his skill with horses which was almost magical. When he learned of the silver mines in Chihuahua, he decided to go there and see about investing in them, for he wished to make a home in this new world."

The priest stopped and Blanco explained some of the words

Lan did not understand. His flesh prickled. Skill with horses? *Alan?* He listened tautly as the priest resumed.

Graeme and his family had fitted out a wagon and started for Chihuahua. They had not been seen again alive and it had been supposed in Brownsville when Graeme failed to write his friends that the small party had been caught by Indians or strayed and died of thirst. He had been all but forgotten when the letter came and spread a furor through the town.

It seemed the Graemes owned lands and great houses in the Highlands and this roving Alan was heir now since his older brother had died without children. If Alan Graeme were dead, his children would, of course, be owners of his estates.

"I checked in Laredo," continued the priest, "and at last found an old muleteer who had years ago found a wagon with skeletons. They were near water and there was no Indian sign so he guessed they died of some illness. The man wore a watch with A. G. engraved on it, and inside his wife's wedding ring were the words 'Alan and Margaret.' That was the name of Graeme's wife. The old muleteer had kept these things in case relatives of the dead ever came hunting them. He brought the skeletons back and they were decently buried. But—there were only two small children. The third Graeme child was missing."

Lan felt hot, then cold, as Father Denis came to him, placed in his hand a ring and a thing that must be the watch. "My boy, since soldiers find many odd puzzles, I wrote all the commanders at frontier forts to see if they had any word of a lad about fifteen, orphaned years ago and possibly reared by traders or Indians. Colonel Schell here responded with the few facts he knew about you—your red hair and blue eyes, that Comanches had raised you after finding your family dead of plague. This all ties in with the old muleteer's story. Even your name, Lan. It could be a baby word for Alan which was also Mr. Graeme's name." Lan felt dizzy and the floor swam strangely beneath him as Father Denis finished solemnly, "My boy, I have every confidence that in your palm you hold your mother's wedding ring, your father's watch."

"It—it is not certain," Lan argued.

"No," admitted the priest. "But it is as certain as anything so hidden by time and death can be."

The watch with the initials, the muleteer's story, even the supposedly inherited hair and eyes—these Lan could have dismissed or refused to credit as proof. But Alan Graeme's "magic" with horses . . . Lan believed. He did not want to, but he did.

As if they might speak, he gazed down at the watch and ring. The ring was small. It would not have fitted Swift Otter's warm brown fingers. Was this all he would know, ever, of his blood parents, these mute souvenirs? It was all like some distant tale that had nothing to do with him, yet the metal objects that had belonged to living, breathing people called out to him. And the sadness of it all was that he could never understand. He would never hear the voice of this woman or this man. The lands far over the water were nothing to him, or that strange name. He felt terribly, utterly alone. For knowing certainly of his real parents raised an impassable gulf between him and his Comanche family. As long as he did not know who he was, he could pretend he was really their child, but this knowledge robbed him of that pretence.

Still, this information and these cold metal objects gave him no new identity while they cut him off from his old one. In that moment Lan tasted the absolute loneliness of being a man, of being a separate individual on the earth, imprisoned in himself. Did all grownups feel this way? And if they did, how could they bear to live? How did they find a meaning, a way to reach out and touch other lives as lonely as their own?

Blanco's hand fell on Lan's shoulder. "Lan. I know this is hard to take in. But think of this. Your father left you his horse-talk voice. That is something. And from what Father Denis says, he left you also the red hair and blue eyes of your line.

You are the living proof of your parents as you are the proof of the love given you by your Comanche parents."

Slowly, Lan shook his head. "I want no other parents." Jerkily, he put down the watch and ring. A pang transfixed him and he said in fury, "Why did you tell me this? I do not want to know! How can I ever be one of The People?"

"I am sorry." Father Denis' voice took on a stern note. "But it was not my right to deny you knowledge or your choice."

"What choice?" Lan asked, trembling like a trapped mustang.

"Why," said the priest, raising his brows in surprise, "you own much property in Scotland. The family would like you to return there. Or, if you don't want to do that yet, you have an uncle who will manage your estates till you come."

"This uncle—can't *he* own the big houses?"

Father Denis stared. "I'm sure he would be glad to. But— Don't make a hasty decision. You don't understand. In the great world, money is necessary."

"My world is here. Whatever I am, I know that." Lan turned to Blanco. "Please—You tell him!"

Blanco said, after a pause, "I think you can write the Graemes and tell them you found Lan, that he is well, that he talks to horses like his father. But they had better run the estates. If the uncle wishes, he could put aside something for Lan." The mustanger's smile was the first seen during that meeting. "Perhaps when Lan marries, his wife can find some use for his inheritance."

The colonel who had been listening to all this with growing impatience, asked Blanco something. When Blanco answered, the colonel blew out his cheeks and spoke at length, with emphasis, to Father Denis who kept nodding just as emphatically.

"The colonel says—and I agree," said the priest, "that this matter deserves more thought. I am visiting the ranchos in the vicinity and will be here several more days. I shall hope to hear from you again, my son."

Blanco bowed, taking leave, and Lan followed his example. There was no use wasting his breath. But he would not change his mind.

Next morning after a breakfast of left-over *gorditos* and honey, the mustangers drifted towards the corral.

"It is the 'catch of the souls,'" Marina explained. "Come see." When all the men had gathered, Blanco called Miguel, Chon, and Lázaro. With them, he entered the corral on horseback.

Dust, turmoil, squealing horses, whirling ropes. In a few minutes, Marina opened the gate. The four mustangers hazed out their roped victims and the gate was shut again. With underhanded throws, the other men brought the horses down by the forefeet, and while they lay struggling to rise, Blanco turned his rope over to Felipe and prayed.

"Our Lord, we commend unto you the souls of our dead comrades. We consecrate these mustangs for their peace."

The kneeling men crossed themselves. The mustangs were let up and taken to an adjoining corral. They would be gentled first, Marina said, and their sale price would return to Brownsville with Father Denis.

"Do many mustangers get killed?" Lan asked.

Marina grimaced. "A gopher hole, a bad rope, low limb, or vicious horse—there are many ways. Sometimes a man disappears and it will be months before his skeleton is found, caught tight in the brush. Once we found a man who had been caught by his neck between his dallied rope and a mad horse. His neck—" She looked sick.

"Do you wish your father would do something else?"

"I don't know. I like it all but the penning. Of course, the catch must be made or we couldn't live. But Father says when we have enough money, we'll stock our ranch and live there. Raise horses instead of hunt them."

Money. That was what he had in that land across the water. The thought of telling Blanco he was welcome to some of it passed through Lan's head, but he shrugged it off distrustfully. Money was a dangerous, tricky illusion, not honest trade goods. He had better just leave it entirely alone. If he got mixed up with that inheritance he might be trapped into going to Scotland. Marina's voice jarred him alert.

"Lan, I want to walk through the Fort, maybe see a lady in a pretty dress. Please come with me?"

What? Walk with a squaw, and to look at other squaws? Lan drew himself up haughtily. Then he remembered the things this squaw had done for him—services he had not been too proud to accept, and gave in.

"I will take you if your father can spare me." Lan hoped Blanco would order him to catch and gentle a mustang as the others were doing. But when Marina ran to her father and asked, the captain smiled and nodded.

"It won't take long to see what's here," he told Lan. "And I don't want Marina unescorted. Most of the soldiers are decent, but a few have no manners."

They passed the corrals, the square with the flag which Marina said was the parade ground. Lan grinned as they passed the small adobe guardhouse. "I remember that place," he whispered. "It smelled worse than a camp during buffalo slaughter." It seemed so long ago. The odor of white men no longer troubled his nostrils. He was like a mustang who had survived the first stages of taming. Only there was a difference. Lan grew tame now in order to go free later.

When they caught the white Ghost— Then Yellow Wolf would get a surprise! In the tents of the laundresses behind the adobe soldiers' quarters, children ran back and forth, pursued by yipping dogs, scattering chickens. A few goats were staked to graze beyond the tents, and two men were building an *jacal*, a house of woven brush covered with the native mud which would harden into a stone-like surface. A sustained downpour would melt the whole thing away, but such storms were infrequent and *jacales* cost nothing but labor.

135

They passed the post store. Lan saw the sutler who had tried to examine his teeth engaged in getting down bolt after bolt of cloth for a critical woman who kept pointing at yet another roll. Lan chuckled with relief. What a fate he had escaped there!

Marina said, "Father told me what Father Denis came for. Weren't you excited, Lan?"

"It didn't seem to have anything to do with me."

She tossed her head and the red ribbon bounced along with the glossy black hair. "Don't be aggravating! You ought to at least go to Scotland. Lan, you could cross the whole ocean, just think! I wish *I* could see those houses."

"So do I," retorted Lan. "Then you wouldn't pick on me."

She laughed, then sobered. "Lan. Aren't you going to keep your mother's ring?"

"The mother I remember is Swift Otter."

"But you can't deny the other one completely!" Tears glinted in Marina's eyes. Her hand closed urgently on Lan's. "She must have loved you. And her end was sad. You should love your Comanche mother, but you can't refuse your real parents their right to live again in you. Keep the ring and watch, Lan. Your children will want them. It will be a strange, wonderful story to them—their grandparents who came across the ocean and died here, but left you."

Unwilling to explain the mute, troubling call of the objects, Lan said, "You can keep them for me. I might lose them."

They were strolling past the adobe row of buildings now, the officers' quarters, Marina told Lan. He gave her a teasing look. "You may have to admire the laundresses' dresses. There don't seem to be other women around."

Right in front of them, a door opened. It was the biggest house in the row. Out stepped a girl. She wore a blue gown that stood out in a circle most fearfully and wonderfully, and her eyes were the same blue, like flowers on the mountain.

At sight of them she gasped, clapped her hand to her mouth, and backed into the house. Lan was still staring when he felt a savage tug at his arm.

"Come away!" Marina's voice trembled. "She—she *laughed!*"

Lan looked at Marina in her divided leather skirt and worn moccasins, glanced down at his greasy and dirt-stained trousers. He did not see anything funny. They had been after mustangs and looked like it. "Laughed?" he asked. "Why?"

Sobbing furiously, Marina stamped her foot. "Oh, you—boy! She laughed because she's got lovely blue skirts that stand out like a bell and I—look the way I do."

She stalked down the road, head so high she could not see the road. Lan caught up with her in time to keep her from tripping over a stick.

"I thought you like being a *mesteñera*," he puzzled. "I thought—"

"You can't think," she said witheringly. "You're a boy. You don't understand!"

While, dumbfounded, he pondered this, she spun away, rushed across the parade ground, heading for the corral. Automatically following, Lan considered the problem. He thought she was acting silly. But she had been kind to him and had only that morning brought Diablito fresh milk before she herself ate.

Let's see, now. She likes the way that skirt stands out—Lan turned around. He forced every thought but Marina's hurt from his mind, marched back, and knocked on the door of the big house.

The girl in blue answered. To her astonished expression, he said in Spanish, "Your skirts—please tell me how they stand full like that." Blue eyes shot sparks as she stood there speechless a moment.

"You—you heathen!" she choked at last, in Spanish better than Lan's. "What a thing to ask a lady!"

"But— I only want to know about the skirt. Marina—"

"That girl in leather? Really!"

Her concluding sniff was too much. "She's prettier than you," Lan snapped. "Worth ten times as many ponies! You wouldn't bring two horses for a bride-price. Too skinny!" She was not, but Lan wanted her to know her way of seeing things was not the only one.

The blue eyes seemed to turn black. The full, wide skirts made a swishing sound like a rattler's whir as she started to bang the door. A man's voice called something in the white man's tongue. Turning from the door, the girl replied, her tone furious.

The colonel came from the next room, buttoning his coat. He glanced curiously at Lan, said, "*Buenos días,*" and began questioning the girl. At her answers, he stared at Lan. Once he laughed, spoke rapidly at her reproachful look. She frowned doubtfully, but at last she faced Lan again.

"My father says you were reared among Comanches and are incapable of realizing how rude your question was. Why do you want to know about my—skirts?"

"Marina thought the dress pretty. I wondered if you would trade it to me for some work—something I could do." Looking in her startled eyes, Lan flushed. What could he possibly make for this fair-skinned doll-woman? A bow? Arrows? He turned on his heel. "I was stupid. Forget it."

"Wait!"

The girl put her hand on her father's arm, just as Marina so often did with Blanco. They talked a moment.

"Father says you are a good horse trainer," she said in a softer tone, smiling a little. "I have only been here a few weeks and cannot ride well. I have a handsome mare but she's unbroken. She should be handled gently. If you will work with her, I'll give Marina a dress and the petticoats that spread it out. You can take them now. No!" Hand flying to her mouth,

138

the girl gave a pleased cry. "The dance tonight! She can come here and I'll get her dressed for it. You go right now, Father, and invite her!" The blue skirt disappeared in a whirl.

The colonel laughed, raised a shoulder, and stepped out with Lan. Lan was glad to get away from the girl. She changed as fast as the color of her eyes. But if she would give Marina those envied full skirts, Lan was willing to break a buffalo for her.

At the corral, the colonel talked to Blanco. The other men were each working a horse, most of them using blankets though a few had tossed saddles on the mustangs and were accustoming them to the burden and smell. Marina, eyes red, came out of her *tipi*. She moved for the corral, a blanket over her arm.

"Listen," Lan called. "Good news!" And he told her of his bargain with the colonel's daughter. "Colonel Schell is talking to your father now," Lan finished. "You're to go to the house and get all dressed for a dance tonight."

"I won't," said Marina flatly. Hurt pride smoldered in her voice.

"But—the stand-out skirts you liked! And I'm taming her mare in payment."

"Then you wear the skirt," Marina flashed. "That *gringa* won't get another chance to make fun of me!" She went to the corral and led out the horse Chon had caught for her.

Hitching it to a post by the hackamore, she spoke to it continuously and began rubbing it with the blanket before she backed off and slapped the blanket against its hide. She would do this till the horse learned that no bad thing would happen. When it was used to the blanket, she would accustom it to the saddle, and at last ride it.

Completely baffled and half-angry, Lan got his own rope and blanket, moved to the corral. One minute Marina wanted skirts; the next she took his head off for supplying them.

It would be a relief to work with honest horses. Them he could understand, but never, in a thousand moons, girl-women.

⊭ ⊭ ⊭ *Tamed Mustangers*

Before entering the pen, Lan selected a horse, a chestnut mare who was far enough from the mass of horses to be caught easily. As a Comanche he would not have ridden a mare except in extremity and Mexicans felt the same way. This was an expression of male dominance. But Lan knew some of the finest, most enduring mounts were mares. He was a little jealous of the whites who would use the best horse they could get whichever it was.

"I'll help you get her out of the pen," said Chon, who, mounted, and with a ready rope, was lending his aid where needed.

He roped the mare and held her while Lan slipped a hair hackamore over her head. Tossing back Chon's freed rope, Lan led her from the corral. When she balked and showed the whites of her eyes, Chon spanked her with his *reata* and she pranced out quickly.

Coaxing her away from the distracting corral, Lan talked to her softly, for even without the magic, a human voice can reassure a wild thing. Aware that some of the men were watching him, he wondered if Javier had told of the loss of his gift. No matter. He could still tame horses though they would not again believe his tone when he called them kin.

Sweating, breathing hard, the mare nervously swung her

head. Lan caught the hackamore where it circled the muzzle and held her still. With his free hand he touched her nose and ears, stroked her eyes, caressed the swelling, muscled neck. After she had learned his smell and touch, he picked up the blanket. When he passed it before her eyes, she shied. He stroked her and repeated the motion.

Next he cracked the blanket across her back, did this till she stood quiet but trembling under the light blows. If Lan were going to train her thoroughly, he would have put her in the corral till next day and worked her again with the blanket, but since Blanco merely wanted the mustangs introduced to men and to being ridden, Lan caught her by the neck and sprang on her back.

He caught a glimpse of the colonel, shoulders discouraged, going towards the parade ground. Marina must have refused him, too, then. Stubborn! The mule was not born who was unreasonable as a girl. Lan had no time to follow his disgust further for the mare took all his attention.

Her method was not to pitch, but tear around in circles, crazier by the second. When she showed no sign of wearing down, Lan bent back one of her ears, kicked her hard in the ribs. She stopped circling, took off in a straight line. This seemed to remove the mad stimulus that kept her going even past exhaustion. In a short time, she slowed. Turning her, Lan talked to her as he steered her back to the holding pen where the partially-broken horses were kept separate from their wild companions. He rubbed the sweat from her with the blanket, slipped off the hackamore and let her trot in to join the dozen horses already there. As Lan started to select a second mustang, he saw a blue figure—with wide-belled skirts—moving towards the corral. He glanced towards Marina, knew by the jerkiness of her motions that she, too, had seen the dance of the sun off golden hair.

As Yellow Wolf would say, *What a scalp!* Any war chief

would be proud of it. Lan decided he needed a drink of water. This was no time to try concentrating on a horse when a more interesting struggle was about to develop. As he went to the water bag at the cart, he kept an eye on the two girls. Marina was still using the blanket on her first horse.

Suddenly dropping the blanket, she set one hand in the mane and leaped up. The horse skimmed off like a bird, making for the wastelands. The colonel's daughter screamed.

"She'll be killed!"

"No," Blanco assured her pridefully. "Wait."

Lan had sipped all the tepid water he could stomach. Replacing the hide bag, he went to the corral. Chon had a dun gelding waiting for him. Lan took him out of the pen and began the blanket work, but he faced in the direction in which Marina had disappeared, and stayed within earshot of Blanco and the blonde girl.

In what was altogether about a half-hour, Marina came in sight on the horizon, her mount still running, but under control. Swooping in a circle about her father and the girl in blue, Marina slid off the mare and started to take her to the holding pen. She acted as if she did not know the colonel's daughter existed, much less stood near.

"Please—" The blue skirts swayed forward and white hands impulsively caught thin brown ones. "How splendidly you ride! I'd give anything if I could do half as well!" A dimpled smile flashed. "I can barely stay on a nice, slow, old mare."

"Truly?" Marina asked, staring in disbelief.

"Yes. You see, I've been in a convent school in San Antonio. Father finally let me join him two weeks ago. My mother died when I was born and an aunt in Philadelphia kept me till I was old enough for school. Oh, it's wonderful to be here! And if you'd come home with me, we could have such fun today."

The quick-sympathied Marina could not frown at the eager, pleading face, but she muttered, digging her moccasin in the dust, "I'm needed here. As you see, there are many horses—"

"The men can handle them." Blanco was smiling broadly. "You go along with the *señorita*. And you may stay for the dance. In fact, I am coming myself."

"But I do not know the *gringo* dances!" Marina wailed.

Blue eyes sparkled. "I'll show you the steps. And plenty of handsome officers will be happy to let you step on their toes tonight!" Arm laced through Marina's, the colonel's daughter was making off with her guest when Marina stopped. She looked, with dismay, at her leather divided skirt.

"Oh, you can—" The blonde girl bit her lip, started over. She had learned to respect Marina's pride. "Would you do me a great favor?"

"What?" asked Marina suspiciously.

"Father bought a pretty mare for me. I don't know how to tame her but I don't want the soldiers to do it, either. They're rough. Now if you, being a girl, could ride her a little and show me what to do, it would put me so far in your debt I could never get out. You'd just naturally have to let me give you one of my dresses. I have a rose one that would set you off beautifully. And Major John's wife has a little rose bush. I know she'd give us some buds to put in your hair. Let's go! We've got lots to do by evening!"

"First," decreed Marina, refusing to budge, "we work with your mare."

The colonel's daughter, used to her own way, looked startled. Then she laughed and nodded. The two girls walked off together, blue skirts by stern leather. Blanco came over to Lan. "You will come to the dance also. The colonel requests it."

"But—"

"More," cut in Blanco, with a nervous tug at his moustache, "I need your company. Miguel, I know, has plans to visit a ranch nearby with Chon so he can't come. You wouldn't expect me to go there alone?"

"You don't have to."

Blanco gave a grim chuckle. "Listen, the colonel is a good man, but no one can properly watch two pretty girls at the same time. You would not want Marina to marry one of the blue-coats, would you?"

Lan had not thought about her marrying anyone. Still, Blanco was right. "If you'll get me some clothes, I'll come," Lan said sadly. He whacked the dun with the blanket, told it under his breath, "You think you have troubles! You ought to be a human."

After supper that night, Blanco and Lan, laden with clothes from the cart, went to the post store and in one of the rooms that served as lodging for travelers, they scrubbed themselves with a strong yellow stuff Blanco called soap, sitting with knees drawn up in oaken tubs. Lan did not think much of this custom, but Blanco insisted on it. "A good bath every few months is even healthful," the captain said. "We cannot go to this dance with the stink of mustangs, sweat, and dust on us. I will not have my Marina shamed."

Though he grumbled, and applied the soap gingerly, Lan did feel better when he had rubbed himself dry with a coarse towel the sutler provided. His skin tingled and the clean clothing was like cool wind on his flesh.

He wore Miguel's fiesta shirt, lavishly embroidered on the lace, and a pair of black velveteen trousers Chon had loaned, a fancy silver threaded short waistcoat of Lázaro. The men had mostly all brought some dress clothes, for they planned to stop in Laredo after selling the last of their summer catches and celebrate a while.

Blanco had to shave, but he was still ready before Lan who had trouble figuring out the clothes and adjusting them. Surveying Lan, the mustanger said admiringly, "You are a handsome one! That red hair goes well with dance clothes. Well, let us pay the sutler for our baths and go." It seemed that the sutler rented his tubs and towels to anyone who was sufficiently desperate for a bath. The soap was free.

"You yourself should not mind going to the dance," Lan grinned. He was sincere in his teasing. Blanco's stark black trousers and waistcoat with their silver trim, his silver-conchoed black hat, and the snowy white ruffled shirt, repeated effectively the black of his moustache, the shocking white of his hair. He looked—Lan tried to think of a word the colonel's daughter might use. Exciting.

They passed several officers and a few ladies as they walked to headquarters. The office had been cleared, banks of artificial flowers hid the desk, and bright lanterns hung from the ceiling. At one end of the room sat four men making music from instruments Lan had never heard before, though one object, played crosswise with a threaded stick, looked a little like Chon's guitar.

Ladies, hair piled high or falling in curls from combs or jewels, plied odd little folding triangles of gaily painted cloth or paper, and laughed at remarks which must have been the cleverest ever made by attentive men. The officers, most of them young, wore gold braid, sashes, and swords that must surely get in their way when they danced.

A choked, trapped sensation rose in Lan. How had he ever gotten into this? He shifted sideways, half planning to leap back out the door, when the colonel loomed in sight from behind a group of joking officers.

He shook hands warmly with both Blanco and Lan. The two older men talked in English a moment. Then Colonel Schell took them around, introducing them to the various groups. Lan could not remember a name. He followed Blanco's example, bowing to the ladies, and murmuring in Spanish. No one seemed to hear anyway; he could have spoken in Comanche.

The women would start making over him before the colonel even finished the introductions.

In their gleaming dresses and jewelry, the women reminded Lan of brilliant-plumaged birds. He tried to quench his awe of them by privately reflecting not one of them could make a *tipi* or dress a buffalo. The officers, now, were not half as impressive as warriors in ceremonial attire, but these women—! Comanche squaws did not use ornaments as much as the men, though most of them kept their faces daubed with red clay. Lan fought back a grin as he wondered how these ladies would look so decorated.

Father Denis was hemmed in by three plump older women. These fixed upon Blanco when the colonel brought them over, and one took Lan's hand, patting it till his cheeks burned and he wanted to sink through the floor. The purple plumes in her hair stirring, she spoke in some length to Blanco, and then, to Lan's utter confusion, she said in Comanche, "Poor boy. I know what you've suffered. I lived captive among those devils for three years."

If she had brandished a scalping knife, Lan could not have been more surprised. This stately, handsome woman, a slave for the squaws?

"You—?" he stuttered. "When?"

"Fifteen years ago. My first husband and I were traveling from San Antonio to Laredo. They killed him, of course." Her voice was toneless and Lan suddenly could believe what she said as a vein throbbed in her temple. Her hand rose to her gray hair. "I'm forty. Fifteen years ago, I was a pretty woman with auburn hair. The peace chief took me for a wife. I wanted to die. So when his first wife beat me, I kicked her and pulled her hair. The chief laughed and gave her another whipping with a pole. She didn't bother me after that."

"How did you get away?"

"Soldiers came to parley and Major Clellan who is now my

husband saw me. He demanded my release. The chief refused. That night the major and another soldier slit my tent and got me away. The Comanches pursued next day when they found me missing. The chief was killed in the fight and none of the others felt I was worth more trouble."

Lan said, "They are my people. I will go back to them soon."

She dropped his hand and turned away. Father Denis said, "Have you changed your mind, lad? Will you come back with me?"

"I can't."

"Ah," said Blanco, interrupting with a sigh of relief, "here comes Marina!"

In through the door came an officer escorting three ladies. One was a tall, white-skinned woman with black hair. There was the golden head of the colonel's daughter. And next to her stood a sun-kissed girl in a dress the color of a rose evening sky with dark hair caught back by flowers. She wore no jewels; she did not need them.

A long-drawn breath came from Blanco. His eyes shone. "If only her mother could see her," he said softly.

The officer brought the women over. Colonel Schell introduced Blanco and Lan. The officer was Major Johns and the tall woman his wife. In green-blue cloth that sheened and shimmered, the colonel's daughter smiled up at Blanco.

"Would you dance with me, *señor?*"

Flustered, but too gallant to refuse, Blanco was led off like a tamed colt. The colonel, Marina on his arm, was taking her around the room to meet everyone, and the dance was under way. Lan escaped gladly to a bench behind a bank of artificial fern.

Dip-and-whirl, dip-and-whirl. This was a far cry from the social dances of the Comanche. Lan's head ached from the noise. He longingly eyed the door but men lounged there. If only Blanco would come back. Sweating palms clenched, Lan crouched behind the greenery and prayed to be unnoticed.

"Lan!" It was Marina, back with sparkling eyes from her tour. "Whatever are you doing there?"

"Waiting to go home!"

"Nonsense!" Laughing, she caught his hand. "Dancing's fun. Come, I'll teach you."

Make a fool of himself before these blue-coats? Have them snigger up their gold-braided sleeves about the white-Comanche? Lan tried to pull free, shaking his head.

"Hurry," she insisted, tugging in earnest.

People were looking. Lan, with his free hand, pried loose her fingers. He said with the cruelty of terror, "I don't need a squaw to teach me anything. Go on, play with your *gringo* friends who stole this country from your people!"

Dark eyes grew huge, glistened. With a downward bend of her head, she turned away. A young officer was instantly beside her, bowing, offering his arm. Marina's chin rose high. She laughed and moved into the handsome man's arms as if she had never done anything else. In a moment she was hidden in the gaily-shifting crowd on the floor.

Angry, sullenly ashamed, Lan hunched miserably behind the stiff, unfragrant ferns. There went Blanco, dip-lifting as elegantly already as ever he had rolled a cigarette or tossed a showy *mangana*. Plenty of the ladies, behind their triangular, folded objects, followed with their eyes the *mesteñero* and seemed to envy his young partner. And here came Marina again. That officer did not need to bend that close to hear her, did he? Lan snorted, so absorbed he did not see the woman beside him till she tapped him with one of the closed triangles. She was one of the plump ladies who had been with Father Denis.

"You speak Spanish, I hear! Capital! I learned it from my laundress. One should really adapt to the region in which one lives, don't you think?"

148

She reminded him forcefully of Thunder Waters' opinionated head wife. Agreement seemed the best way out of this. Lan nodded.

"Splendid." She drenched him with a smile. "I knew you were an intelligent boy the moment I saw you. Don't you dance?"

"No, *señora*," replied Lan, drawing back as far as possible.

"Then it's time to learn! A handsome young man who can't dance is a crime against all women. Come, I'll show you!"

Lan crouched away. She rapped him again with the slatted triangle thing. Lan slowly dragged himself up; he figured she would keep hitting him with that ridiculous doubled paper till he did. Besides, he was tired of being forced. He had said he could not dance. Now he would show her!

With amazing agility for one her size, she avoided his feet. "After thirty years practice nothing smaller than an ox can crush my toes," she informed him, maneuvering him with steely fingers. She wore steel strips either in or beneath her dress, too. They cut into Lan when the crowd pressed them close. Steel was in her voice, also, though it was sweetly covered.

"Father Denis tells me you won't return to your white people. Even after they've gone to such trouble to find you."

"They—don't seem like my people."

"How silly! They're your own blood kin. Don't you realize what you're refusing? Houses, lands, a proud name?"

Lan looked over her shoulder. "I want medicine, a name among Comanches. That is all."

"We all have heard how that Comanche who was on the raid left you to face the consequences alone. How can you think of going back?"

"I am not a dog to run to one lodge because he was kicked from another."

The music stopped before she could launch a new attack. A

light hand fell on Lan's arm. He turned to stare down at the colonel's daughter.

"It's time you danced with me," she said. As the music started, she somehow fitted herself to his awkward clasp. They moved off as if propelled by the disapproving look of the older woman.

"My name's Mary. I know yours." Dimples showed as the girl stole a glance at Lan's recent partner. "That's Mrs. Trowbridge, the surgeon's wife. I imagine she was planning your life for you?"

Uncertainly, Lan smiled. "She tried." He was glad he had had some practice so that he had not yet trod on Mary's feet. Dip-swing, dip-swing. He concentrated till a fine dew of perspiration stood out on his upper lip.

"It's too exciting, your being a Scottish heir and all that," she said. "I've read all Sir Walter Scott's books about that country. In fact your whole life's an adventure! Tell me about the Comanches. Was it just terrible?"

Abruptly, Lan released her. "It was wonderful," he said. Unable to stand any more, he walked out between the men at the door. Long after he rolled between his blankets he shuddered like a roped mustang. Live with those people over the water? Or these folk at the Fort? Never!

⚡ ⚡ ⚡ *Track of the Ghost*

Three days later, after a final attempt to persuade Lan, Father Denis began his journey down the Rio. He insisted on leaving the watch and ring with Blanco for safekeeping. "You will want them someday," he told Lan, who muttered embarrassed thanks. He liked the young priest, appreciated his efforts to do what he thought was a favor. But why could not people understand that their good was not always another's?

During the week and a half the mustangers camped at the Fort to gentle horses, Lan saw little of Marina. She was usually with Mary, teaching and being taught. Blanco, though pleased with her happiness, was rueful.

"I have always wished she had girl friends," he said. "I thought it would help her grow up. Now she becomes a lady too fast. *Ay,* what will she do in a mustangers' camp? Soon, soon, I must start ranching."

Lan thought of the Scottish money. He wished Blanco could have some of it: But— No, it was best to forget the whole thing. If those determined relatives across the water heard from Lan at all, there was no telling what they would do.

When the mustangers were ready to move out, Mary Schell came on her gentled mare to tell them good-by and Marina cried at the parting. She kept turning to wave till finally the

151

colonel's daughter was only a toy figure on a toy horse in the distance. Then, swift as the changing wind, Marina's femininity departed. She challenged Miguel to a race, beat him, and then vied with Chon in singing desolate love songs with a laughing chorus after each doleful verse.

Lan was wary of her, though. The rose dress with slippers and petticoats was in a chest in the cart. This Marina in leather concealed the girl who had charmed the wits from all the young men at the Fort. He gave brief answers to her questions, till she frowningly reined close to him.

"Your manners haven't improved since the dance. You were terribly rude to both Mary and me."

"I don't like dances."

"You could learn to. I'd never been to such an affair, either, but I got along."

"You certainly did! Those grinning, bowing officers! The whole bunch wasn't worth one Comanche brave."

Marina's lips curved in a smile. "Really? Well, Lieutenant Strang, the one I danced with first, had just returned from a patrol. He had only five men but they defeated a raiding party of twenty braves."

"Brave women or children?" Lan asked sarcastically.

"He was also given medals for heroism against the Apaches."

"He had better get medals so people will know he's a soldier. Otherwise they'd never guess it."

Pretending not to hear, Marina said, "He also asked me to marry him—after a proper courtship, naturally."

That jerked Lan erect. "How many horses will he give your father?"

She glared. "I'm not for sale. Civilized people don't trade women for ponies!"

Stung, Lan said, "That must be because your fathers are glad to get rid of you and your husbands don't think you're worth much." The old Marina would have slapped him. This new one smiled coolly and said in a superior tone as she rode away, "Children say childish things. Till you grow up, I truly don't wish to talk with you."

She did not, either, as the days and miles passed, though she was merry and sweet with the others. Lan told himself savagely that he did not care. But he did.

Several of the mustangers rode ahead always, watching for horses and having an extra care for any group that might be Guero's. Four days from the Fort, a good herd was sighted.

No white stallion grazed with it. Blanco waved his men on. To Lan's questioning look, the captain said, "My band earned good money off the horses we sold to the colonel. We owe it to you to find the Ghost so that you may choose your own trail."

A moon-and-a-half had passed since Lan joined the mustangers. By now, the young braves would be organizing their fall raiding parties and those who were not going south with them would be moving northwest to set up the village and prepare for the buffalo hunting later. Lan had been over the country now traveled by the mustangers and he knew he was not many sleeps from the winter camp of his people. He thought of Swift Otter who must mourn him as dead, her hair hacked off and jagged cuts on her face. And he thought of Yellow Wolf.

Javier's voice broke into his memories. "We need fresh meat. You and Miguel go get some. Why don't you see how your bow works?"

Glad of a change, Lan nodded agreement. Javier had made the sinew bowstring while at the Fort and Lan had feathered his arrows and tipped them with metal heads which the Fort blacksmith made for him. While Miguel coaxed the loan of Chon's carbine, Lan climbed in the slow-moving cart and rummaged out his bow and arrows. The two boys left the band, riding ahead and to the side.

Miguel glanced curiously at the arrows in the quiver Javier had made. "Why," he asked, "are the two black lines straight and the two red ones spiral?"

"It keeps the shaft from warping."

"Oh." Miguel sounded disappointed at such an ordinary reason. "I thought they meant lightning or something. I'll bet I can bag game faster than you. Guns are better than bows."

"As long as it takes to load them?" Lan derided.

"Wait and see," Miguel laughed.

They rode through high grass and occasional thickets, came to a clearing where water, from the looks of the caked mud, evidently stood during rainy seasons.

"Look!" Miguel pointed.

Skeletons of two deer, torn apart and scattered, lay locked by the horns. Lan rode up close enough to touch the joined antlers. "They were fighting and couldn't get untangled. They must have starved or died of thirst."

"I think coyotes and wolves tore their legs and haunches while they still lived," Miguel speculated. "See how the hind legs are broken and gnawed? They were probably fighting for a doe. Now both of them are dead."

There was a stirring in the bushes. Intent on beating Miguel to the shot, Lan readied his bow, reached for an arrow. Three things happened in a split second. A stag broke from cover, Lan sent his arrow at it, and the whir of a rattler came from the ground. Friend jumped sideways in time to spoil Lan's aim, but not in time to avoid the lightning strike of the ugly flat head. Before the snake could slither away, Miguel's shot tore it in two. Kicking the pulped ends out of the way, the boys swung down to examine Friend's leg.

"If we had a chicken—" Miguel wished. The split warm meat would quickly suck out the venom.

"Well, we don't!" Lan was already making cross-cuts with his knife over each fang mark. "Quick, cut me some tips from that

Spanish dagger yonder." Lan sucked the mixed blood and poison, spitting it out.

Miguel was back in a few minutes. Kneeling, he helped Lan stick the sharp points all around the bite. "When we get to camp," Miguel said, "Javier will fix him up. But maybe this will keep him alive. You ride behind me."

Holding Friend's reins, Lan bumped along behind Miguel. "I got my arrow off fastest," he said. "But I'm glad you had Chon's carbine!" They caught up with the mustangers as night camp was being made. Javier's grumbles over their failure to bring game subsided as soon as he heard about the snake. He drew out the Spanish dagger tips, and brought a small tin from the cart.

"You acted wisely, but this salt will keep down swelling and lameness." The old man rubbed the fine white grains into each cross-cut. Friend endured it patiently and limped only a little as Lan led him to water. Lan wanted to bring his horse some grass, but knew it would be better for Friend to move about grazing and keep the leg active.

Next morning, though, Friend limped till Lan decided to ride one of the bell mares, humiliating as it was. She did not like it much better than he did, and poked sulkily at the rear of the band. When Lan drove his heels into her ribs, she laid back her ears and tried to clamp her yellow teeth on his knee. She might be ridden, her behavior said, but it would be on her own terms!

"*Hola!*" It was Marina, cantering back, eyes dancing as she said in serious voice, "Ah, forgive me, I did not know you were going to a funeral."

"It may be this old mare's," Lan snorted. But his heart lightened. He was glad Marina was willing to be friends again.

She laughed, turning her black mare. "Come with me. We'll get you a fast horse."

"What do you mean?"

They had come up with Miguel who was scanning the horizon. Outlined on a small rise were mustangs. "It's a small group, about six or seven," Miguel said. "Chon and Lázaro will help us run them past Marina. Then you'll see there are advantages to weighing only eighty pounds!"

"You mean she'll catch one of the mustangs?" Lan asked incredulously. "I won't let her. That's too dangerous!"

"I love it," said Marina, tossing her head so that the hair streamed. "Father thinks it's a good idea. If we come on the Ghost, you'll need a fast horse."

Joined by the two older mustangers, Lan and Miguel rode towards the mustangs, cutting back in order to come up behind them. Marina rode to a clump of brush and waited. The bell mare, picking up the excitement, loped after Miguel.

Swinging behind the mustangs, which had already broken into flight, the hunters chased them toward Marina's concealment. Lan hoped she would choose the big *grulla*, the mouse-gray, who seemed to skim over the ground. As the fugitives neared, came level, she rode from hiding, running with them.

Lan held his breath as she crowded the *grulla*. For a while they stayed side by side. Then, smooth as a floating leaf, she set her hand in the big gray's mane and switched mounts. Seemingly unaware of her, the *grulla* surged on. She noosed her short rope over his head, made two quick loops around his nose. With this improvised halter as her only control, she sped on with the wild ones. Lan could never think of her as a squaw again.

"She's done this before?" he asked worriedly.

Miguel, catching up the black mare's reins, nodded. "For sure! When we want only one horse from a bunch, she gets it. It is necessary to be very light for this, very skillful. That is why young girls do it best. I am already too heavy. I slow down the fastest horse till he cannot overtake an unburdened mustang that is any good."

Their part done, the four rode back to the band. The bell

mare resumed her drag position, going slower than ever as if to make up for the recent exertion. Lan kept glancing back. Soon he saw a dot on the plains that grew into Marina on the gray. Lan dropped behind to wait.

His gray hide black with sweat, flecks of lather spotting him, the *grulla* was under Marina's domination. She sprang down, flushed and breathless.

"He's all yours," she said. "Do you want to saddle him?"

While she soothed the mustang, Lan took the saddle from the mare and put it on the trembling gray. "I won't use the bridle yet," he told Marina. "That is, if you'll let me use this rope halter."

She nodded, took the bridle he had slipped off the mare. "I'll put this in the cart for you," she offered.

Lan swung on the *grulla*. "Many thanks," he grinned. "Did I tell you? You looked pretty in that rose dress!"

"Well!" She frowned through a pleased smile. "Must I catch a horse for you before you'll admit the truth?"

The gray was skittery but controllable, even with the light halter. Lan was glad he did not have to use a bit which would have cut the horse till he learned to obey the reins. This way Lan could save the bridle till Grulla, as he called the horse, was able to follow the pressure of knees and reins. By night Grulla seemed resigned to his fate, but Lan still hobbled him. Friend was better, but not in riding shape. Lan talked to him after supper and split a handful of corn between Grulla, Friend, and Diablito. The colt had thrived on the milk at the Fort and bounced everywhere with great self-confidence.

"Breaking will come as a shock to him," Javier chuckled, slipping the colt a taste of brown sugar. "He thinks he is a mustanger!"

The next day they found the moist new droppings of undisturbed horses feeding on familiar range. "You ought to put a bridle on," Blanco warned Lan. "If we meet a herd, that *grulla* may forget he's a man's horse now."

"I will, if he acts nervous," Lan promised. "But I hate to use a bit while he'd still hurt his mouth on it."

Blanco shrugged, riding on. It was only a few minutes till the mustangers rode over a slope. Down in the valley grazed a white stallion. On the opposite slope fed his mares, a dozen of them. Not many could follow the Ghost, pursued as he was by men. Blanco raised his arm to hold back his band.

"The Ghost!" came from many lips, a whispering wind. This was the sought-for dream, the great stallion whose escapes were legendary and sung in ballads. To have a part in catching him would be fame and life-pride to every man here.

But Grulla did not care for Blanco's signal, the tug Lan gave the halter. What Grulla saw were mares—and a rival.

Ears skinned back, heedless of Lan's pulls and kicks, the gray tore down the hill. Momentum pitched Lan forward and he felt the cinch give. He had kept it loose on purpose to spare this beast and now he might die for it. Leaning forward, Lan bit clear through the gray's ear.

Shrilling, Grulla veered his head around, grabbed Lan's knee. He tore off leather and some skin. Lan clubbed his fist down as hard as he could on the mustang's nose. The gray straightened out, running again and Lan saw they were almost on the Ghost. Having no wish to die between two stallions, Lan slid off, catching the saddle horn in a mighty wrench as he did.

The saddle, as he had hoped, came loose. Lan rolled with it through the curly mesquite grass. The stallions screamed as he found cover behind a big *retama* thicket. Bruised, gasping for breath, Lan peered through the thorny limbs.

Tails straight out, the horses ran past each other, stepping high, whistling through distended nostrils. So this was the Ghost!

Proud-crested as a war chief, muscles rippling under the

smooth white hide, this was truly a king stallion. Still Grulla, not yet filled to maturity, followed instinct and challenged. Rearing on their hind legs, they walked like medicine dancers in jerky cadence, feinting at each other. Then all ability to follow them as separate forces vanished, for they struck with their forefeet, lunged for the jugular with their bared teeth, taking whatever hide and flesh they found.

Red welts rose on both, staining the white coat, darkening the gray. Lan could clearly hear the vicious click of teeth coming together. Grulla was getting the worst of it, but he fought wildly, butting at the Ghost, squealing as he rose high and lashed out with sharp hoofs.

Besides growth, the Ghost had experience on his side. He would have fought many upstarts like the gray, knew every trick. Spinning, he kicked wickedly with his hind feet, knocking Grulla in a heap. While Grulla struggled to rise, the white stallion slashed down at him with maiming, cutting blows, whirled to kick again with his back feet.

In this moment's respite, Grulla lurched up and fled. His ambition to own a herd was all gone. The Ghost ran him over the slope, taking a strip from his rear every few jumps. Satisfied with that, perhaps scenting the mustangers, the white stallion returned to his mares, hustled them off to the west.

Blood pulsing to the beat of the white stallion's hoofs, Lan came to his feet, staring after the vanished herd. He was still like that, in a daze, when Blanco pulled up beside him.

"We watched from the slope. You're lucky you got off in time."

"I lost Marina's rope. Unless we catch Grulla—"

Blanco laughed. "We won't. He'll run till he drops. The rope will rot or work off in time and won't keep him from grazing, so let's forget it. Friend isn't too lame now. Throw your saddle on him."

Javier helped Lan affix a new cinch for the broken one. Lan

hardly knew what his hands did. *The Ghost,* he kept thinking. *The Ghost!*

"What will we do?" he asked, catching up with Blanco.

"Trail slow and easy. There's a corral about two days from here, beyond that butte you can barely make out to the far west. If we try to chase him now the Ghost will simply make fools of us."

Miguel fingered his rope. His eyes glowed as if with fever. "The great stallion," he breathed. "And all we have to do is catch him!"

"Just catch him," Blanco echoed with a grim laugh. "Mustangers have been saying that for five years. But none of them have."

"Did you ever come close—this close?" Lan asked.

"Several times. Once four of us ran him across the Rio. When our horses were whipped and we half-dead, we came back to our camp. Next day, too tired to chase, we saw him on his old range near the Frio. But the closest I ever came was back when he was still a youngster, running alone. Of course he was not famous then, but he had promise. I saw him go into this narrow draw to drink and I waited, for he'd have to come past me to get out. A water-logged horse, as you know, is much easier to catch than one without the added weight. As he came by, I tossed my rope, caught him neatly. It was when I made the dally that my horse spooked, shook me off. The Ghost made away with my best hair rope." Blanco grimaced as if he still felt the chagrin. "Since then he has had to change his graze many times and dozens of ropes have whirred near him. But he still runs free."

"Maybe," dreamed Marina, a glint of exaltation in her eyes, "I could catch him."

Blanco shook his head. "No," he said violently. "The best *mesteñera* of the Border was killed trying that leap to his back. Her two brothers took up the hunt. Both were trampled to death." Looking to the west, the captain spoke softly, with pain and sadness. "I have a feeling about the Ghost—that he is the last great wild one, that with his capture the days of the mustangs and those who live by them will be numbered. We will fall on tame days of lesser horses, lesser men, while the ground shrinks under us like a green hide. The Ghost is your people, Lan, and me, and all the wild ones. Therefore I do love and grieve for him. He cannot run away forever."

An ache throbbed in Lan's throat. His flesh prickled and he cried angrily, "If you feel that way, why will you hunt him?"

"Why does a man live, knowing each day brings him nearer death?"

Beneath his anger, with sudden pain, Lan recognized the same struggle in himself. But the Ghost was the price of his freedom. He had no choice, had he?

That night, Miguel, Lan, and Chon kept on the track of the mustangs, wearing them down. From time to time they saw the dim sheen of the Ghost on a moonlit slope, the darker silhouettes of his mares. Lan grew so sleepy he kept coming to himself with a jerk. Only by remembering the Ghost was up ahead —the price of his own freedom and vengeance on Yellow Wolf—could he stay awake. At earliest dawn, Marina rode up.

"The others will trail now. You three sleep. Javier has food for you. Rejoin us by evening. You'll night-trail again then."

Three sleepy riders ate and slept soundly in spite of the sun sifting through the mesquite fronds above their heads. They woke in the heat of early afternoon, drank from their canteens, and saddled their freshened horses. Javier had gone on with the cart.

"Listen," proposed Miguel with an estimating glance at the sun. "There's no hurry. Let's try to get a deer."

"And have the luck you did last time?" Chon teased. "Well,

I'll save you boys further humiliation. I'll bleat one close and surely one of you can hit it."

"Since when could you call up the deer?" Miguel scoffed.

"Since I got this from a soldier at the Fort," said Chon. He produced, with a flourish, a small bone instrument. "*Ándale!*"

Leaving the track of the mustangers, they found a clearing which, from the tracks, was an animal crossroads. Loaning Miguel his carbine, Chon waited for the boys each to prepare their weapon.

"Which will win?" he asked dramatically. "The bow or the carbine? Step up and see, good people!" Raising the bone to his lips, the mustanger blew till it made a sound like a bleating fawn. Had Lan not seen, he would have sworn a lost fawn was piteously calling its mother.

After about five minutes a doe entered the clearing, slowly, head up, stopping frequently. The wind was in the other direction and she did not smell the men. Coming forward on dainty hoofs, she looked distractedly into the brush. She was only yards away, an easy shot. Why did Miguel not get her? Lan tensed his arrow.

But the eyes of the doe swung towards him. Large and dark, they were like Swift Otter's. Lan had killed does before, but never like this, through one's love. Dropping his bow, he shouted. She was gone in an instant.

"What—?" cried Chon, starting up.

But Miguel, too, wiped off his forehead, handed back the carbine. "I'll never kill a doe like that," he said. Chon, growling, rode on ahead.

Lan looked solemnly at Miguel. "Did you see?" asked the Mexican boy. "That deer had the eyes of Marina. How could we kill it?" Lan shook his head.

"I saw my mother." They rode knee by knee a while. Lan finally remembered what he was searching for. "There is a song, not of my tribe, but my father taught it to me. He had it from a Papago.

> Upon the mountain the dying quarry
> Looking at me with my love's eyes . . ."

Were they fated to hunt that which they loved and destroy it? Deliver the mustangs to the whites, to the tamed world? It burst in Lan's heart like a war song that he could not help turn the Ghost over to the colonel. The Ghost must run free.

"Let's hurry," Lan said. "I have something to tell Blanco."

⚹ ⚹ ⚹ *Horse Talker*

They found the mustangers making camp in the last blaze of the sun. Going straight to Blanco, though his feet tried to drag, Lan said, "Please, let's—not chase the Ghost." Blanco turned slowly.

"We do it for you."

"I know. But listen—" Lan gulped. Could he really go through with this? Even if it worked, if Thunder Waters surrendered the horse and Lan went free, what good would that be when the Comanches would never accept him? They would consider his asking for the horse as almost treachery, as what might be expected of a white renegade. Yet as Lan's tongue stuck on the hard words, he knew that if he helped capture the Ghost he would, in his own heart, by himself, be branded a traitor. "Perhaps I can get back the white stallion Yellow Wolf rode away. The colonel would rather have his own horse than a wild one, wouldn't he?"

Blanco tugged his moustache, pondering. "You mean to steal it from Thunder Waters?"

"Not unless I have to. I will find Thunder Waters, tell him how I was tricked, that the horse is his only through a fraud—and that I, who stole the stallion, claim the right to return it for my freedom."

"Hai!" Blanco whispered. "Thunder Waters is a man of

honor according to Comanche beliefs, but he won't like that. Even if he lets you take the horse, you will not be welcome again among The People."

Lan's throat ached. He forced himself erect. "I know that. But at least I can see my mother and she will know I live."

Blanco was silent. Did he think Lan might not come back? Pride kept Lan from insisting on his honesty, but it was hard to keep from fidgeting. Blanco finally looked up. "It is your choice. If you would lose your place among The People for the Ghost, I will not stop you. Still, in case you fail with Thunder Waters, we shall continue on the Ghost's trail." Lan gazed toward the north.

"The camp should not be much over three days' ride from here. Give me a week."

"We will camp here," Blanco said, "and try to keep the Ghost in the area of the butte by riding circles wide around it. There is water below the butte, a branch of the Rio, so neither the mustangs nor our camp will go without water. There are quicksands, though, so if you come back that way, watch for them."

Miguel, who had listened to all this, said, "I would go with you, *amigo.*"

"No, Monkey." Lan spoke with tightness in his throat. Why, it was hard to say good-bye to these people he had at first hated! "I lived with the tribe and even if they are angry with me, they won't kill me for my parents' sake. But it would be different for you. You watch the Ghost, eh?"

The news spread among the men. They came up to wish him good luck as he got jerky and corn from Javier. The old man sighed. "Has it come to you that you could simply stay with the Comanches and not return at all?" He nodded in proud satisfaction. "No. I see it has not." Lan grinned.

"You keep my bow and arrow, wise one. After the way I

worked on it, you know I'll be back!" Marina had to hold Diablito to keep him from running after Lan. Some distance from the camp, Lan glanced over his shoulder and saw them, still standing there.

All night he rode, following the North Star. He knew that if he kept a northward course from the Rio, he would come to the east-west flowing river along which Thunder Waters' band would be. Having explored the river part of every year for the past twelve, Lan was confident of finding the village once he struck the river. His heart swelled inside him.

He would see his mother. That he would do first of all. And Yellow Wolf—he would be called to answer Lan's charges. How his long jaw would drop, how he'd stare! And if he wanted to fight, Lan was ready.

But beyond that? Bitterness, a sick feeling mixed with Lan's already confused emotions. If Thunder Waters gave up the horse, if it were safely delivered to the colonel, what could Lan do then? After claiming such a forfeit from the chief, Lan could not live again with The People, even if he had retained his horse-talk voice. He had lost that, he never had possessed medicine, and demanding the white stallion for an enemy would make him near to a renegade.

Go over the water to those houses of the Graemes, he could not. Blanco was his friend and would keep him, but Lan would never get the stench of the Saint James corral from his nostrils, forget the broken bodies or the betrayal of the black stallion. He could not be a mustanger.

Shove these thoughts from his mind as he would, they were always ready to confront him. Sleeping only when overcome by weariness or when Friend began to limp from the snake bite, Lan made good time. He ate in the saddle, munching the dry foods, sipping from the canteen between water holes.

At mid-afternoon of the third day, Lan reached the river at a bend where, in winter hunger, he and the other boys fished, breaking the taboo on such creatures. Food rules were strict, but the law of hunger overrode them. He should reach the village by dark.

Turning west, he followed the winding, shallow water. By sundown he could make out the *tipis*, marched around the big square in the middle. He wanted to come in after twilight so as to escape notice. Dismounting, he rubbed Friend's healing leg and rested a while. Then he stripped down to the breech cloth he had continued to wear under his mustanger's clothes. Before he mounted, he rubbed himself with mud and Friend's sweat, to kill any un-Comanche odors he had. The village dogs were noisy and he did not want them alerting the town.

He hitched Friend beyond the village and came strolling through the lanes as casually as if he had never been away. A few children, playing late, did not give him a second look. Grouped about the center square where Thunder Waters' official lodge was, were the other *tipis* in regular streets, about two hundred of them spread over several acres of land. The familiar woodsmoke and horse odor filled Lan's nose, along with the indescribable acrid human smell. The mustangers were not exactly sweet-smelling, but Lan, with a disloyal guilt, caught himself thinking he could have located the village a mile off by only its stench.

As the widow of an important chief, Swift Otter's home was on the first row of tents facing the square. Less important families occupied the *tipis* radiating backwards. A man's position could be judged by the size of his *tipi* and its location. Each of his wives, if he had more than one, would live in her own adjacent *tipi* with her children. Pausing by his mother's lodge, Lan saw a portent that made him frown.

By Thunder Waters' living quarters grazed the white stallion. That showed how highly the chief prized it. He would probably have preferred to part with one of his four young wives. Lan set his jaw, lifted the flap of his mother's tent, and stepped in.

"Mother," he whispered, kneeling by where her bed of hides was. "Mother, it's Lan."

Her arms were around him before he could finish speaking. Patting him, holding him close, she said brokenly, "Are you a ghost, my son? I do not care if you are! You have come back! Oh, my Lan—" Lan stroked her hair. It smelled of orrisroot and oil. But even pressed to the warmth of this person he loved best, he knew he was not her son, he was not Comanche. The past weeks and a ring and watch from two dead people had worked past the layers of consciousness into his being. As a child, his adoptive parents' love had made him part of their life, but it no longer could. He felt as if his heart were breaking and he stood in a cold wind that stripped away every shred of a name and identity from him. Life was the wind and he did not know if he could stand before it. He gasped as he touched the short, spiky ends of his mother's hair. Yes—and she had gashed her cheeks. He could trace the scars.

"Mother!"

"I thought you were dead," she sobbed. "When no sign of you was found at your vigil, we were sure a spirit or animal had taken you."

"It was Yellow Wolf," Lan said harshly, hating his enemy twice over for Swift Otter's disfigurement. "What did he tell The People when he came back with his bride-price, the blue-coat chief's horse?"

"Bride-price? What are you speaking of, my son?"

"That white stallion by Thunder Waters' lodge. Did not Yellow Wolf trade it for Thunder Waters' daughter?"

Swift Otter shook her head. "Yellow Wolf brought the horse to the chief, surely. But it was for damages. The day after you went on your medicine quest, Yellow Wolf carelessly shot one of Thunder Waters' mounts. The chief was already disgusted with Yellow Wolf for acting as he had with you. So, as is an injured person's right, Thunder Waters demanded reparation. He made the task one to sober even Yellow Wolf—the blue-coat leader's great white horse."

Angry blood hammered in Lan's forehead. He clenched his fists. "Why, that's worse than ever! Yellow Wolf *had* to get the horse. I'm going to find him now, not after I see the chief!"

"What do you mean, Lan?" Swift Otter's hands shook him a little. "Yellow Wolf is not here. He is on a raid. Now explain!"

Hoarsely, Lan told her how Yellow Wolf had offered him the bait of winning honor, how he, Lan, had talked the stallion to the gate and been betrayed by Yellow Wolf. Briefly he explained his bargain with the colonel and his present mission.

"That evil Yellow Wolf!" cried Swift Otter. "I never trusted him! These mustangers, they have been good to you?"

"All very kind except one, a bad white named Inglés. He is no longer with us."

"Inglés?" Swift Otter repeated. Fear quickened her voice. "Two bad white men have been here. With presents, and a story of mustangers who are being paid by the blue-coat chief to raid us."

"What were these men like? Did you see them?"

"Several times. The whole village buzzed with them. One was red-haired, with a scar. The other had yellow hair and cat eyes." She shivered. "His horse was marked as if by a lion's claws."

"That's Inglés!" Lan exclaimed. "He marks his horses that way. He lied about the blue-coat chief. Did the warriors believe him?"

"Some did. The wife of Thunder Waters told me the young men shouted and were glad when the yellow-haired one finished speaking. He said that if some of our warriors would help kill these mustangers, they could have all the plunder, scalps, and a good rifle apiece."

Lan felt as if his blood had frozen. "And how did Inglés explain his—generosity?"

"Thunder Waters' wife told me the white claimed to be a Comanchero and a friend to The People who did not wish to see his customers destroyed."

"He wants revenge," Lan muttered, stunned. Shaking his head to clear it, he got to his feet. "When did he leave? Who went with him?"

"Yellow Wolf and twenty young warriors. The glory alone was promise enough. They left early yesterday. Inglés says the mustangers are headed for a butte close to the Rio."

"He spied on us, saw the route of the Ghost, and knew we would be penning near there," Lan calculated. "That gave him time to come here. Were he and Guero alone?"

"They said these mustangers had killed their companions."

"Hai! The crew must have refused to work for them any longer." Lan thought rapidly. "They will rest nights and travel slower than I did, coming alone. It will take them five days to the butte." Lan swung towards the flap. "I will go to Thunder Waters, ask for the stallion. On it, I can warn my friends. We can make some sort of a defense."

Swift Otter stood up. "I will go with you to the chief."

"No, my mother. I will speak to him as a man. And then I must go quickly." She reached her hands up to his face.

"My son, you live. Now I am happy. But I feel it in me that you will not return to the Comanches to live." She swallowed. "Maybe you will come to see me sometimes, though?"

Eyes stinging, Lan pressed her hands. "My mother, you will surely see my face. I will come when I can. But you speak truly. I am not one of The People." The flap did not drop down as he stepped out; he knew she knelt in the opening, watching him go. It was harder than if she had reproached or wailed or begged. Only the need of his friends camped unsuspecting near the butte gave Lan the strength to walk on.

Outside the chief's *tipi*, Lan paused, asked for admittance. Thunder Waters himself, face slack with disbelief, lifted the flap. Lan spoke quickly.

"I did not die on my vigil, great chief. I come to ask for justice." He told the whole long story, including the lie of Inglés about the peaceful mustangers, then waited in respectful silence, though his blood raced with impatience, for the old man to weigh his account.

At last, Thunder Waters said, "I believe you. The stallion was gotten by you, not Yellow Wolf who owed me damages. Take the horse, buy your freedom. Now—" He frowned, plainly arguing in his mind, before he threw back his shoulders. "Listen. I will go with you after the warriors and forbid them to fight. I have no love for mustangers, but these were friends of yours. Evil sat boldly on the foreheads of the whites and I talked against the raid, but the young braves were eager."

Already the chief had motioned one of his wives to make ready provisions. "Tell her to fetch a *maana* hitched near the river a half-mile east," Lan said. "He is my horse, a good one. Take him as my gift."

"Then I will give you a saddle for the stallion," Thunder Waters said. With his own hands, he saddled the handsome white beast, but put his own gear, including his best bow, on a rugged pinto. "Since he is not mine, I will not ride the beauty." Lan saw Swift Otter, a shadow in the darkness, watching as they rode away.

It was well both that Lan had been raised in the saddle and that the stallion had become used to Comanche riding, for Lan, exhausted from three days and nights with little rest, kept drowsing off. They stopped at mid-morning and slept till early afternoon, then took up the southern trek.

Rested enough to start reviewing the situation, Lan cleared his throat. When Thunder Waters noticed and looked at him,

Lan asked, "Oh chief, the whites must have spied on the mustangers. But how did they know where the village was?"

"The one named Guero knew," the chief said grimly. "Last spring he came with Comancheros to trade for hides. I thought then he looked more like a thief. And long ago I saw this Inglés in a Comanchero camp. But I heard later they had run him off for bringing the authorities down on them."

"He was with Blanco for quite a while." Sudden dread squeezed tight fingers around Lan's heart. How could he have forgotten? Or been so stupid as to let Thunder Waters come with him? The chief knew Blanco by another name—Small Man.

The truth had best come now than later. Lan gulped. "Thunder Waters! Blanco, who saved me, was once your captive. The blood brother who got away—who was so brave."

Grim, high cheekbones hardened, wide nostrils flared. Thunder Waters had forty scalps and one of his ceremonial shirts was trimmed with choice ones. Lan was afraid, but he insisted. "Blanco is my friend."

"Small Man ran off long ago and hurt no one in his escape," Thunder Waters finally conceded. "I will forget—because your father was my comrade—that Small Man ever lived." Lan smothered a sigh of relief. It was sunset before either spoke again and then it was the chief.

"You are not coming back to The People?"

"I do not belong. I could not get medicine."

The old man sighed. "Perhaps your father's spirit kept the medicine animals back. He knew it could not help you in the days to come." A chill traveled up Lan's spine. To hear Blanco speak thus was one thing; it was quite another to hear it from this warrior whose name was great among Comanches.

"What do you mean, Thunder Waters?"

The chief gazed into the sunset. It painted eerie red on his bronze face. "I do not say this in the village, son of my old friend, but I see it. The white men push us from all sides. They will put us on little squares of land and bring us meat when they have killed our buffalo. Our sun goes down. In its last light we hunt and raid and dance, but the dark will close on us soon. There is no help. I have used all my medicine and the Great Spirit does not hear me. We shall die from mange and sadness like caged wolves."

"Do not say that!" Lan cried. The old eyes rested on him, full of pity and devastating knowledge. Lan bit his lip and was quiet.

Munching dried meat and pemmican from the chief's supplies, drinking from Lan's canteen, resting when they must, the strange pair worked steadily south. It was a dream to Lan, a fevered frantic nightmare, as he rode the white price of his freedom, trying to save his friends. Before him, too, was Yellow Wolf, the liar, the betrayer.

At noon the third day they saw the distant butte. As they came nearer, two white clouds rose, one of these dividing again into two as they approached. Lan shielded his eyes.

He could make out dark figures now, in the dust, two of which were horsemen, the third, mustangs. And, yes, there, driving his mares, was the Ghost!

Lan set heels to the white stallion. As they swept at an angle towards the runners, Lan guessed at what had happened. Blanco's men had been distance-herding the Ghost and his band when Inglés' attack forced them to close in on the mustangs. And now it seemed that Inglés, too, wanted the Ghost, for instead of shooting at the mustangers, his men were crowding the wild horses. They probably hoped to rope the Ghost before he could escape and then turn their attention to Blanco's poorly-armed crew.

Suddenly, as Lan neared the side of the butte, the Ghost cut through his mares. They scattered. Unencumbered with them, he ran now by himself, straight for the butte, because

173

men were at either side and in back. Lan rode furiously, trying to reach the rim, to turn back the great mustang. He was pounding close when the Ghost pulled up short on the brink.

Glancing back, the stallion saw pursuers all around. His muscles bunched. He gathered himself—beautifully, purely, a wild harmony of flesh and muscle—and leaped off the cliff.

For a moment he seemed to fly, mane and tail spreading. Then he plunged. Lan, hauling up the colonel's horse, jumped from the saddle, and looked down. The Ghost struggled in slime. The quicksand Blanco had warned against! Heedless of his skin, Lan half-slid, half-fell down the butte, and ran to the edge of the bog.

The Ghost's thrashing had carried him neck deep. His eyes fixed on Lan's like a cry of wildness, like the death of all he loved. Lan cried out, "Brother, brother!" It was the sound, the secret voice.

Raising his ears, the stallion struggled, but it was too late. The eyes held Lan's as if comforted and Lan called, tears blinding him, part of his heart sinking down forever with the horse, "Brother, brother—death gives you peace—" Never to be chased again, coveted, or hunted. Never to be tamed. Run on, white Ghost, run free.

Trembling, unable to look away as the mud closed over the white head, Lan did not mind the sounds above till a voice shouted in warning. Turning, he swerved in time to avoid Guero's bullet, but Yellow Wolf was fitting an arrow to his bow. Almost in the same instant, the two fell from their horses. Guero tumbled down the butte, lay still by Lan's feet, his neck broken, a bullet in his heart. All Lan could see of Yellow Wolf was one arm dangling over the cliff, but Thunder Waters had come in view above, and Blanco was by him.

"Come up," they shouted, one in Comanche, the other Spanish. Lan thought how strange it was to understand them both. He hurried around to the side of the butte and came up the slope. When he got there, Thunder Waters was addressing his warriors who sat shamefaced before him.

"Take up the body of Yellow Wolf. We will bury him that his family be not shamed, as I killed him that our honor not be. He would have killed this boy whom he had already tricked and betrayed."

The carbine in Blanco's hands showed who had disposed of Guero. Inglés sat his saddle with his hands crossed, weaponless.

"This time," said Blanco, "you go to the Fort and Army justice for inciting the Indians."

"I restored your daughter," whined Inglés. "You can't forget that!"

"Why don't you kill him?" demanded Thunder Waters who had not understood the Spanish exchange. Blanco explained. The chief snorted.

"Your daughter is about fifteen?"

Blanco nodded, puzzled. "Then," said Thunder Waters, "I think I can remove your gratitude. I last saw this man with Comancheros about twelve years ago. He had with him a little girl dressed in red with a cross about her neck. The Comancheros were going to sell her to an old *hacendado* who had lost his only child, a girl about her age. But I learned later that the Comancheros drove this Inglés away when they found out he had not found the child with Indians as he claimed, but had killed her mother and stolen the girl. The Comancheros found an orphan for the *hacendado*. It would seem this white man thought his best course was to play hero and return the child to her real father, who would gratefully support and defend the benefactor."

"What's he saying?" cried Inglés, mouth contorting. "What's the old fool yammering about?"

From a mask-frozen face, Blanco's eyes burned like flames. He raised his carbine. "You—you killed my wife?"

Inglés wheeled his horse. "Red devil!" he screamed. "How did you know?" He sprang from the saddle, trying to drag the old chief down, knife flashing in his hand.

Blanco's carbine spoke in the same instant that an arrow from Javier, shot from Lan's bow, pierced the blond through the chest. He died before they could reach him.

That night they camped and ate together, mustangers and Comanches. Next morning as the Indians got ready to leave, Blanco came to Lan who stood by the edge of the butte. As they looked at the quicksand, Thunder Waters joined them.

"Will you go now with The People?" Blanco asked. Neither he nor Thunder Waters had given any sign that they remembered each other. "If that is your wish, I'll take the colonel's horse to him."

Speaking in Comanche, Lan said, "I do not know where to go. I am not a Comanche, but the name beyond the great water is nothing to me. And I cannot be a mustanger, either. Not after the Ghost—"

"Son of my old friend," said the chief sternly, "instead of saying what you are not, tell us what you are."

Startled, Lan thought a minute. Then his lungs filled with air and he put back his shoulders, feeling the sun in his face as when two long moons ago he had asked it for strength.

"I am the chosen son of Arrow In His Shield and Swift Otter, I am a friend of Thunder Waters. Also I am the friend of Blanco, and Miguel and Javier. I have kept my word to the blue-coat chief. And the voice, the horse-talk, has come back to me."

Thunder Waters nodded. The shade of a smile touched his lips. "You are a man. That is enough for now, and even always, Talker With Horses. Keep your word and be faithful to friends. You are welcome in our village when you come; and do not worry about your mother. She will not want for anything."

"Tell her—" For a moment Lan could not speak. "I will come to see her. Thank you, great chief."

The warriors rode, a long thin line of The People, seeming to dissolve in the morning sun.

"Lan." It was Marina's voice. He turned to find her standing by Blanco. Miguel, too, had joined them. The girl's cheeks were flushed and she held her father's hand caressingly. "Lan, we aren't going to mustang anymore! Are we, father?"

Blanco shook his head. "The Ghost decided me. We have some stock, more can be raised, and after we take the stallion to the Fort, we go home to our rancho. For good. Will you come with us?"

Thunderstruck, Lan gazed at his friends, and realized they meant it. "I'll come!" he said so hastily they all laughed. Miguel twirled his rope in a gay spiral.

"We'll have plenty of excitement keeping off thieves and chasing our herds," he grinned. "*Ay, ay, el Rancho Grande!*"

Lan took a last look down at the bog. He said to Blanco, "Is it permitted to light candles for a horse—I mean, as you do for men with the *lazo de las ánimas?*"

"For the Ghost?" Blanco gazed over the plains as if he saw something—running, running, vanishing in the wind. "Yes, I think it might be."

Diablito nickered and ran alongside as they saddled and rode, east to the sun.

CPSIA information can be obtained at www.ICGtesting.com
Printed in the USA
LVOW090413010612

284216LV00001B/23/A